KIDNAPPED BY THE MAW

LAYLA STONE

PROMPT PENWORKS

CONTENTS

THINGS YOU NEED TO KNOW BEFORE STARTING THIS BOOK:

The alien races and places you will be exposed to in this book are:

- The Outworlds is a section of space that is not governed by the military known as the Federation. The Outworlds are less organized as a whole filled with races with abnormal abilities.
- Cerebrals are an Outworld race with natural telepathy and telekinesis.
- Boores are an Outworld race with a great sense of smell and can turn into shadows.
- Semps are an Outworld race that can teleport.
- Ratas are an Outworld race with a great sense of smell and long life.
- Numans are a Federation race of highly intellectuals that have been known to experiment on people without guilt or remorse in the name of science.
- Demons are a Federation race once known as Kirca. There are four types: Night, Roth, Silk and Red.

They are mostly known for making underhanded deals, unethical behavior, and having an unbreakable spirit.
- Terrans are a Federation race once known as humans from Earth.
- Graches are a Federation race with addictive hormones that they use to snare a mate.

ONE
PIRATE ATTACK

With a tap of a button on the console, Amaree powered on her sloop. The ship's engine hummed, and the navigation screen illuminated. On her right, she tapped the Minky screen and logged into the quantum network. Opening her active medical contracts, she updated the file with the patient's information, clarified the original ailment, and added in her medical solutions before closing the contract.

The Minky home page expanded, and she saw two missed calls from her mother, one message, and zero medical contracts available. Leaving the hospital to be a traveling doctor hadn't resulted in as active a lifestyle as she'd thought. Not to mention the lack of planets with access to the Federation system to request medical help.

The home screen disappeared as an incoming call popped up.

Her mother.

Again.

Taking a breath, she accepted the call to see her mom shifting anxiously and impatiently. Her mother was part Kooyan, and that race did everything at full speed. Therefore, her mom, who had already called numerous times, was probably at the end of her patience.

"Hey, Mom," Amaree greeted as she programmed a flight path from the Fultrim Moon to the Sarem Moon, which was on the other side of the Asaiah System in the Outworlds.

"Hey, Ree, quick question."

"Yeah, what's up?" Amaree said as she pulled on the ship's controls and lifted off the landing dock.

Shifting in place, Sasha, her mother, asked, "On a scale of like, one to ten, how bad is it if someone is glowing purple?"

Trying to keep a smile from her face, she asked, "Does this person have micro-purple flakes floating around her skin, or is this person's skin emitting purple light?"

Her mother held up a finger and walked away from the screen. Amaree heard her mom say, "I have to see... Look, you're literally throwing up your guts. I'm trying to help you...no, my daughter isn't going to tell anyone. She's a doctor...of course, she's Federation-trained. Look, do you want to find out how to stop glowing or what?"

Amaree engaged the autopilot and sat back to cross her legs, fighting the desire to laugh. How her mother always found some emergency to get involved in was a talent from Seth of Stars.

When her mother didn't return quickly, Amaree added, "There's a new tab out of Lotus Adaamas called a Purple-fairy-flight tab. It makes you glow purple and messes with your equilibrium to make you feel like you're flying. When the chemicals wane, the user goes through several hours of motion sickness. Symptoms include vomiting, dizziness, blurred vision, dehydration, and a series of dark purple spots on the tongue that never go away."

Sasha's blond hair bounced as she jerked her head sideways into video range. The disappointed frown was exaggerated when she repeated, "Never?"

"Nope."

"That's ridiculous."

Amaree shrugged. Lotus Adaamas was a Demon port planet known for many exciting and entertaining things, but as a doctor, Adaamas was the drug planet. Whatever scientist had created the thousands of tabs making their way through society deserved to be caught and sent to Debsa, the prison planet, so he or she couldn't do any more harm.

To her right, Amaree's navigation screen chirped as a ship represented by a blue dot entered her flight space. It wasn't on the Federation flight path, or it would have been directly behind her. The indicator slowed and moved to the rear as if deciding to join a flight path.

Unlikely.

Narrowing her eyes, she reached over and zoomed in to the ship to get a better look at what was following her.

"What? What's wrong?" her mother asked, moving farther into the video frame.

Faking a professional calm, Amaree said, "Nothing."

"I know that face. Your father gives me the same look when he doesn't want me to worry."

Ignoring her mother's astute comment, she turned off the autopilot and took control of her ship. "How did your friend get a hold of a Lotus Adaamas tab? Koho, the inspector, checks every cargo shipment that comes into the Sarem Moon."

Her mother gave her a look that said: *good question*. Leaving the video again, Sasha talked in a quick, low voice.

The ship that was following her was closing in. Initiating the weapons system, Amaree selected the long-range torpedoes and waited to see if the other ship was just messing with her or if they intended to do her harm.

As a doctor, morally, she couldn't take the first shot.

Sasha slid back on screen. "Are you sure there is no way to get the purple dots off the tongue?"

"There is no medical cure on the market, and because it's not a known poison or toxin, a medscope won't fix it."

Sasha winced. "What about the glow? How long will that last?"

Amaree pressed her lips together, trying to remember the exact time while keeping tabs on the ship that moved out of the Federation flight path into a parallel trajectory as if planning to pass her. "Uh, three days, I think."

Amaree heard a female curse.

Sasha snapped her head to the side and shushed the person. To Amaree, she said, "You need to make something to fix this."

Amaree wasn't Ansel, her brilliant Numan mentor, who could whip up something to fix non-documented ailments. Amaree was a good doctor with excellent precision in procedures and identifying diseases, but she would never be a person who advanced the medical field. "Adaamas' tabs aren't something I can cure. Cures aren't whipped up like cakes."

Sasha gave her a pointed look. "Ree, it's Amy."

Oh, good Seth of Stars.

"Hetten Amy, or Human Amy?" Sarem had two Amys, and they were both walking disasters. Both were fully functioning bodies with the intelligence of a half-eaten grape.

"Human Amy." The mortal was a beautiful nineteen-year-old hairdresser with a soft heart, big dreams, and no common sense to save her from a slew of boyfriends who took advantage of her. Considering that Sarem was a small moon town of only five hundred people, Amy would probably have attended a docking party.

A lot of Federation cargo ships with young workers stayed through the night and enjoyed *visiting* with the locals. Amaree no longer had to guess where the tabs had come from.

"I can look to see if someone added something to the announcement, but no promises," Amaree offered.

"She needs help before her parents come home. She said they already warned her that if she left the moon again, they would send her to live with her aunt on Port Meno."

Amaree wasn't surprised that her mother was helping someone to break the rules. Her mom was a lot of things, but a strict rule follower wasn't one of them. Sasha believed that a little danger was good for the soul.

"Port Meno's very pretty, lots of waterfalls," Amaree said as she reached over and targeted the other ship. The blue dot crept closer and closer. In a few minutes, it would be within range for her to get an accurate shot off.

Whoever was flying behind her had yet to ping her ship's general communication system, so they obviously didn't want to chat.

"You hated all the bugs, and I remember you telling me that if your aunt and uncle didn't live there, you'd never step foot on the planet again."

"Their mutated mosquitoes leave massive welts. I was having a bad day," Amaree defended. "Human Amy might actually like it."

"Nooooooooo. She's the best colorist on the moon," her mother whined.

Amaree rolled her face towards the navigation screen, hoping her mom thought she was just rolling her eyes. She selected the target and discharged the first torpedo. The ship used its flares and deflected the attack. In return, it shot two her way.

Pushing the throttle up, she barrel-rolled down and hit the flares to keep the torpedoes from following.

"What are you doing? You're not even paying attention to me. This is important, Ree. She needs your help."

"Did you even ask Human Amy if she wants to stay on the moon? Because last I heard, you told me she was done with all the men on Sarem."

Amy cried from the background, "You told her?"

"I didn't tell her about anyone in particular. I just asked Amaree why she didn't date any of the guys from the moon," her mother lied.

Amaree knew about every single one of Human Amy's boyfriends. Her mother was a big liar.

Targeting the attacking ship, she fired two more torpedoes. Instead of flying away from the bigger ship, she turned around and zoomed in on their hull.

Her mother stepped back into view, expression one hundred percent mother-mode. "Do I need to call Ansel?"

A low blow, but not low enough for her mother to use a guilt trip. "He's not my mentor anymore. I'm a fully certified doctor."

"Yes, you are. And yet, I have a medical emergency, and you aren't even willing to try. If I have to call Ansel, I will."

"Last I heard, he wasn't taking calls," Amaree said, firing another torpedo. The ship deployed it's countermeasures.

"He talks to Sci."

Ansel had retired when he, her dad, and her uncle had a big fight over lost memories. Ansel claimed that some of the memories he'd lost affected his ability to work in the medical field, so he built a workshop to create helpful bots—or something like that.

Calling Ansel was the wrong thing to do, and her mother knew it, which was why she pushed.

"Fine, I'll do it," Amaree said as the bigger ship discharged a close-range EMP burst. Her sloop's lights on the bridge switched from white to red. The floor lights started blinking, letting her know that the ship was using its backup power source. Which also meant, it was time to stop playing nice.

As soon as the Navigation screen came up Amaree cursed, as five more torpedoes were seconds from impact.

The call with Sasha reconnected. "You're the best daughter ever," her mother cooed, and Amaree ignored it as she rolled the ship, releasing her flares.

"I'm the only daughter you have. And I'm going to go so I can do some research." Without a goodbye, she disconnected the call and watched as the bigger vessel deployed a smaller ship.

"Oh, no, you don't," she snapped. If the other craft's envoy was able to breach hers, she'd be screwed. "I'm not interested in being kidnapped today."

Centering her screen so she could see both ships, she used her telekinesis to grab the incoming envoy and push it back to the bigger one's bow tubes. Using her unique ability with metals, she connected with the alloric hulls, liquified a small portion and fused them together. Now if the bigger ship launched a torpedo, it would either blow up the envoy or backfire into the weapon room.

She waited to see if the ship took off or hailed her. After two minutes, nothing happened, so she figured they had enough. She grabbed the controls, pulled her sloop around, and continued home.

TWO
AM I BEING KIDNAPPED OR RESCUED?

Amaree walked into her lab and headed to the chiller to get a Niffy, when she spotted her mother on a swirl seat, curled over the counter with a Minky pad. The sound of an electronic ping sounding meant her mother was playing another speed game.

She grabbed herself the drink and walked to the opposite side of the counter, popping the top. The game buzzed, and her mom snickered at her score, then looked up and said, "Finally. What took you so long?"

"It's not a straight flight home," Amaree said, keeping all thoughts of what'd happened away from her mind. Being on Sarem Moon meant being around telepaths. The population was a mix of Federation races and Cerebrals.

Cerebrals were her father's race—beings with telepathic and telekinetic abilities. Being a hybrid, she was telekinetic but couldn't hear anyone's thoughts. Not that she wanted to.

"How long do you think it's going to take?" her mother asked.

"A while. I don't even have a sample of her DNA to work with yet. Nor the tab."

Her mother reached into her side pocket and pulled out a

handful of something. Placing whatever it was on the counter, Amaree noticed a tube with a swab inside, next to a small, purple-and-blue bag with a yellow, purple, and blue, one-inch by one-inch tab.

"Okay, now how long do you think it will take?"

Amaree had no idea. "How much time do I have?" she asked since her mother was being so insistent.

Checking the time on her Minky first, her mother answered, "Twenty-two hours."

Impossible. Even though she'd looked over her old notes and assignments, the breakdown process would take her at least three days. "I'll see what I can do," she said, picking up the tube.

It took nineteen hours of struggling to break down the basic information on Human Amy's DNA and the tab to realize there was no way she could figure it out. As a last option, she called the one being she trusted to answer the phone. He also worked in the Federation. Typing in his Federation ID, she held her breath.

On the second ring, the Minky screen widened, and a handsome Red Demon smirked at her. "Pretty sure you just made my day, Peaches. What's up?"

"Pax, I need to know how to contact Arvey." She winced, worried that Pax would know that she'd failed as a doctor and needed help.

Somehow, Pax looked like he was laughing at her while simultaneously appearing disappointed. "Sure, I can help. But I need to know what happened first. Can't just call me to use me for my contacts."

Pax was a Weapons and Tactical Response Commander. He had gone to battle numerous times and had once been used as a fighting slave. He was well over a hundred years older than Amaree and had gone through so much, yet he was the sweetest guy she knew.

He always knew how to make her smile.

"I have two hours to help cure Human Amy's purple-spotted tongue, and I'm not even close to figuring it out."

Pax leaned back and laughed. "Did I just hear you refer to someone as 'Human Amy?' Is that a new medical term?"

"We have two Amys in the city. One's Hetten, and the other's Terran. My mom was the one who coined the term, *Human Amy*."

"Right, blame your mom," he said, tilting his head to the side as he pursed his lips. "Actually, I can see her doing that."

Amaree smiled in agreement.

"All right, Peaches, I'll help you out," he said, tapping the desk. "But you have to promise to call me more often, okay? Or, better yet, come and be our doctor on the ship. Vivra would love to have someone she can trust."

Amaree had no idea that working with Vivra and Pax was an option. "Really? I thought you would have had academy-trained doctors."

Pax leaned forward and pointed at the screen, "First of all, you're Federation trained, too. By the best doctor we've ever had. Also, Vivra and I were talking about you the other day. We'd love to have you. Are you thinking about it?"

Yes. No. Yes. "Maybe," she said, tapping her thumb on her thigh, liking the thought of leaving Sarem Moon but not liking the idea of being a doctor on a ship where she could fail the entire crew if they came up against a strange disease.

"Let me know when you're ready to transfer over. I'll pick you up myself," he said before tapping the side of the video and then adding, "Okay, I'm transferring the call to Arvey."

"Bye," she said before rubbing her hands on her thighs, more nervous now that she was calling the guy she had seen at the family get-togethers. She'd never actually talked to him. He always came across as someone who didn't like her.

He answered on the fourth ring, and she saw a dimmed cabin with Arvey standing in black boxers with wild and unruly hair, rubbing his eyes. "I hope someone is dying. Otherwise, I'm going to be pissed."

"Oh, uh..." Amaree whispered while seriously thinking about terminating the call.

Arvey dropped his hand and looked at the screen. At first, he just stared, and then cleared his throat. "Amaree?"

She held up a hand. "Hi. I'm...really sorry. I didn't mean to wake you, and I would have already terminated the call, but I need to ask you one simple question."

Arvey grabbed a pair of pants and pulled them on. "Yeah, sure, anything. What's up?"

It was hard to focus when he wasn't wearing a shirt. She had always thought him attractive and brilliant, and this call would ensure that he never saw her as a real doctor. But she needed his help. "I have two hours to make a cure for the aftereffects of the Lotus Adaamas Purple-fairy-flight tab. I'm having trouble recognizing what chemicals broke down the DNA in her tongue to keep the purple swollen lumps."

He nodded and then wiped his mouth. "Do you want me to walk you through the sequence of how to find it? Or do you want me to send you the cure compounds so you can just make it."

"She's Terran, does that make a difference in the cure's ingredients?"

"No." He snorted.

Hating that he was laughing at her ignorance, she politely said, "Yes, please send the cure."

He reached up and touched the side of his Minky screen. A minute later, he told her, "Sent."

"Thank you," she said, biting the inside of her lip. "I'm really sorry I woke you up. I promise this was a one-time thing."

He opened his mouth as if he might say something but then stopped and took a deep breath. "Glad I could help."

"Me, too. Bye."

He didn't say anything, just terminated the call. Feeling less confident in her skills, she opened her messages and read what she needed to do and got to it.

A little over an hour later, she left the cure on the counter and sent a message to her mom, letting her know that it was ready. Instead of going home, she went back to her ship. She needed to get far enough away that the Cerebrals didn't hear her emotional reflections.

She left the landing pad for the orbiting docks—the long, metal disk that encircled the entire moon.

She checked to see if any other medical contracts had popped up. Nothing. Deciding she might as well get an overhaul, she put in the request and sat back in the pilot's chair. It would take weeks to fix what the EMP had done. Plenty of time for her to figure out if she would take Pax up on his offer.

She was honestly ready for something different—something more.

Her Minky screen pinged with a call from a most unexpected person. Accepting it, she sat forward to look at her cousin—a face she hadn't seen in over eleven years. He looked so much like her uncle, it was incredible. Even the yellow eyes were identical.

"Kava? I...how are you?"

"Everything's good. You busy?" he said from what looked like a captain's chair in a large ship.

"Nope, I just orbit-docked my ship for repairs. I've got nothing but time."

He leaned on the arm of the chair. "Good timing, then. Wanna go for a ride?"

Remembering old times, she grinned. "Depends, where ya going?"

"The black zone."

She sat back, laughing nervously. "It's full of pirates. As in the *really bad* pirates. No one goes past the asteroid belt."

He tilted his head. "You afraid?"

He knew better than to ask her that. "One-on-one, no, I'm not afraid of pirates. But you're talking about an area of space that's completely untouched by the Federation. It's without law. No one knows how many ships there are."

"Technically, there are laws, just not Federation ones," he said casually. "But that's beside the point of my call."

Right, the call to go for a ride into the black zone. She wanted to see him, but she didn't want to go anywhere dangerous. "Kava..." she started, ready to explain her reservations.

Sitting forward, he spoke firmly. "I haven't seen you in years. You have nothing to do, and you know I can keep you safe. Come on, I'm pulling up to the dock next to you. Get over here."

Kava was one of the most powerful Cerebrals on record. He could keep her safe. She didn't doubt that. But years ago, her parents had warned her that Kava wasn't in a good mental place. They'd said it was because he had been let go from the Federation but they didn't say why or tell her more. Then, a few months ago, they'd said he was better and working again.

Not knowing what had happened concerned her a bit.

"Why are you going into the black zone?" she asked.

"To steal something valuable from the pirate queen."

Folding her arms, she was already mentally putting the

brakes on something so dangerous. However, telling him, "*No*" could be bad. So, instead, she said, "Stealing is beneath you, Kava."

He chuckled darkly. "We're stealing back a Federation commander who's being held hostage."

Shocked, she slammed her hand down on the arm of the chair. "The word is *rescuing*, Kava. Not stealing."

Kava shrugged. "Same thing."

"No, it's not." Shaking her head, she stood up. "I'll be right there. I just need to get some things."

"I'll be at the ramp. See you in a few."

The call terminated, and Amaree hesitated because she realized that she'd agreed to go into the black zone to rescue someone. It would be dangerous, and she was already doubting her decision.

THREE
CANNIBALS NEED TO EAT, TOO

Gammon tried to wet his tongue, but it was no use. His parched mouth wouldn't produce anything to quench his thirst. He bit off the loose skin from his chapped lips and spit it out in all directions. His stomach burned from lack of food, and his limbs were numb from being tied down.

Starving brought out the worst in him. The longer he went without food, the more he re-lived the things he'd done when he lived in hell for over a hundred years. At this point of delirious hunger, he'd eat anything—dead or alive.

Taking in a deep breath, he pushed against the cable keeping him immobile. When he exhaled, he tried again to shift his legs, feeling the skin give way but not enough for him to escape the tension. A growl reverberated in his chest, followed by the shuddering hiss unique to his race.

A hint of charcoal hit his nose, and he stopped struggling. Only one person smelled like that. Resuming his arrogant displeasure, he waited as the pirate queen unlocked the door and pushed the thick metal panel open.

The darkness in the room dissipated as she stepped inside. He winced as the bright gold light her body emanated burned his eyes. The air warmed, and his skin prickled. At first, he hadn't known what that meant. But after months of enduring her visits, he'd discovered that it was because the light her skin gave off removed all the moisture from the air.

The queen sauntered into the room, flipping her long, gold hair over her exposed left shoulder. She wore an off-the-shoulder dress, white with little crystal teardrops dangling everywhere, tinkling as she moved.

The garment was short enough that he could see the gold panties she wore beneath, though it did nothing to rouse the male part of him.

He was utterly turned off.

The pirate queen waved her hand in front of her nose. "I don't get how one person can smell this bad. Didn't I have you hosed down a week ago? You are the smelliest Grach I've ever known."

He wasn't a Grach, not even close. But his race looked like them, though they had significant differences. Gammon didn't correct her because he had been posing as a Grach for over a hundred years while working for the Federation.

"I suppose I should have you hosed down again, but I don't want to lose another man."

She had plenty of idiot pirates in her asteroid city. She could spare another one. Gammon was hungry, and he'd delight in eating anything he could. The pirate queen placed a hand on his thigh and leaned over. "But if you tell me what I want to know, I'll give you two of my men."

He opened his mouth to say she should go to hell, but all that came out was a hiss from his dry larynx.

She snickered.

"You know, if you just gave me what I wanted, your time here would be very different."

She was a big, glowing liar. She kept him to get the specifics of his last mission.

Running a finger over his arm, she whispered, "If you wouldn't have broken out of every single cell I put you in, eaten the other prisoners, and destroyed my pods, I might have offered you a spot in my kingdom. You seem like the kind of male I could depend on."

Her kingdom? Gammon didn't think anyone would see her rotting space city as a *kingdom*. The portion of space she controlled was bleak and savage. At times, even her pirates attacked each other.

The pirate queen's eyes raked down his body, and he could smell the change in her scent. She liked what she saw, but she—like all the smart females in the universes—didn't appeal to him. Thankfully, as a Grach, most females were hesitant to enter into an intimate relationship.

"You're resourceful and smart, and you could make a good living as a captain."

He tried to speak again, to tell her that he'd eat rocks before he ever agreed to work for her. Gammon could see the same soullessness in her that he had seen in the Red Demon who'd put him through hell.

"I love how expressive you are. You don't hold anything in." Huffing, she stood straight. "It's too bad you won't take my offer. Things will only get worse for you now, and I won't care when you come begging for me to take you in."

Gammon started to cough, his throat too dry, his saliva not wet enough.

"You deserve your misery," she said, shaking a finger at him. "I've thought about burning you myself. Using all the anger I have and just...searing your skin, cooking you from the outside in, but I figure the smell would reek so badly, I may never get it out of these walls or my clothes."

Sauntering to the door, she said, "Just remember...what happens to you next is your fault."

Gammon didn't feel even a glimmer of fear. She could do nothing to him that would change anything—nothing in his life could change the dead part of him.

Two males came in a while after the queen had left. The little light from the hall didn't do much to aid Gammon's vision, but then again, he never needed great sight. His sense of smell could direct him in the dark.

The first male walked to the back, and the other reached down to grab the two front legs of the chair Gammon was in. As soon as the seat started to move, Gammon pushed his feet down as hard as possible. The male dropped the front of the chair with a yelp. He shook his hand and then used his other to punch Gammon in the jaw.

The impact was strong, and the nerves in his face burned. Blinking away the sting, he watched the next two hits come, unable to fight back. His pain receptors screamed, and he growled.

"You done?" the male behind Gammon asked his attacker.

The male with the red knuckles pointed a long finger. "Kick at me again, cannibal, and I will break your face."

Been there, done that. Lived through it.

A hand wrapped around his lower jaw from behind. The pain from earlier came back as small fingers dug into his skin. "Shut up and grab the chair."

The idiot in front did as directed, but his hold was weak, and Gammon toppled over. In the confusion, the male holding him from the back got his arm too close to Gammon's mouth.

The male tried to move, but Gammon was faster and able to catch two of his fingers.

Biting down, he crunched through flesh, sinew, and bone. Warm liquid coated his tongue and throat—for which he was grateful.

A high-pitched male scream rented the air.

"You sick bastard." The male, now two fingers short, cursed before pulling out a phaser and pointing it at Gammon's chest and pulling the trigger. The projectile was an electrical plate that landed hard on Gammon's chest, burning through his shirt and sizzling against his flesh. White-hot electricity shook his body.

The same male put away the phaser and asked, "Now, are you going to keep it up, or do you need another dose?"

Gammon took a second to hold up his head and take in a deep breath. Then, he opened his mouth wide enough for both guards to see the fingers. He moved the *food* with his tongue and started to chew.

The guard with the missing digits jerked forward as if he were going to throw up, then ran out of the room.

"You're one nasty bastard." The other guard walked to the back of the chair and kicked it so Gammon's face slumped to the side.

Then he grabbed the back of the seat portion and lifted, carrying Gammon upside down. On the way out of the cell and down the hall, the guard didn't hold him up very well. His face scraped the surface of the wall several times, making his already bruised and worn skin start to bleed.

A long twenty minutes later, the guard finally let go of the chair, once more letting Gammon's face hit the floor before shutting the door. Blood ran freely from Gammon's body, hitting the floor. The deep throb he felt made all thoughts dissipate.

Gammon jerked as the guard shot him again with the phaser as he cut him from the chair. The burn shook his body so violently, he felt numb, and his limbs didn't seem to respond to his mental commands.

Grabbing him by the armpits, the guard dragged Gammon towards a long, reflective slab. Gammon tried to curl his hand with each tug, yet nothing happened.

The guard turned him face-down and stabbed him with something in the armpit. His back bowed, and a rush of blood to his limbs made him tingle.

"The queen wants your nasty gramones so she can infect those who betray her."

Oh, hell. *That* was why he was being stabbed? Was that a needle?

His limbs came back to life as the guard pulled out the syringe. Gammon rolled and wrapped his legs around the male's waist, jerking him to the floor. Grabbing an arm, he pulled it back until it was almost out of its socket, then opened wide and bit down, tearing the flesh to make it hurt more.

The guard fumbled with his weapon. Gammon let go and scrambled for the phaser. Following the scent, he grabbed it and shot the male twice. As soon as the body hit the floor, Gammon checked for a heartbeat.

None.

With his mouth coated in blood, he knew his voice worked again. Clearing his throat, he suspected the room was recorded —like the rest were. "In two hours, I'll be ready for a snack."

FOUR
MASTER OF MASTERS

Amaree buzzed with excitement. She was doing something incredibly foolish and dangerous, and yet she couldn't say no—not when she could witness her cousin saving a life.

Kava stood at the top of the ramp with a half-smile.

With a little bounce, she raced up and thought about hugging him but figured it might be odd since they'd never hugged before. Holding in her excitement, she rocked on her heels as she held her traveler's bag. "Long time, cousin."

"Long time," he agreed as he pulled her into a hug, surprising her. She dropped the bag and embraced him. It was warm and quick. "You cut your hair."

Touching a strand of curls, she said, "Yeah, it's easier to deal with the curls when it's short."

"It's also darker."

"Colored it," she said, touching her hair again. "Human Amy said it's a better contrast for my blue-green eyes."

He chuckled. "Human Amy."

"My mom came up with the name."

"Aunt Sasha would," he said before shaking his head. "I

noticed Douglas the Deadbeat isn't on the moon anymore. When did he leave?"

Amaree grinned. "My mom ordered paper from another moon, just to put up flyers around town stating how bad of a ship mechanic he was. Put him out of business in less than three months."

"Did you ever tell her that *you* melted the engine casing and that it wasn't Douglas?"

She snorted. "Do I look like I want to die? She loves her ship. Plus, you and I both know Douglas *was* a deadbeat. He charged for working on ships that he never touched, then told the owners it was beyond fixable. He deserved what happened."

"Yes, he did," Kava agreed before reaching behind her to push the button for the ramp to close. He didn't wait to make sure it was sealed. Instead, he used his chin to point towards the cargo bay. "Come on. I'll show you to your room so you can put down your stuff."

Picking up her pack, she slung it over her shoulder and followed, about to comment on how conspicuous the ship's red color was, but two figures near a series of boxes drew her attention. The male had dark grey skin, black hair, and red eyes. He knelt on one knee in front of a little girl with the same color skin, hair, and eyes.

"Those are Boores," Amaree whispered in awe, noticing how gentle the male was while inspecting a little brown bear that had white tape over one ear. All the stories she'd heard about that race said they were ferocious. But there was nothing savage about a father talking to his daughter.

Wait.

She turned to Kava. "He talks?" she asked, knowing that that race didn't talk. They didn't have the vocal cords for it.

"He was a fighting slave for a Red Demon who implanted a

vocal box or something like that. I'm not a doctor, so I don't know the particulars."

Amaree was instantly curious. Turning back, she saw the little girl take back the bear and then issue a high-pitched scream that hurt Amaree's head. Wincing, she covered her ears. In her mind, where she knew Kava could hear her, she said, "*Obviously, the girl didn't get a voice box.*"

Kava spoke into her mind. "*Nem, her father, was no longer a slave when he met and mated. His daughter, Kye, will need a voice box one day. She already gets frustrated because she can't make the same sounds as her parents.*"

Oh.

"I can make her one. I used to make them for my dolls."

Kava gave her a look before once more turning in the direction they had previously been walking. In her mind, he said, "*Those weren't dolls. Those were creepy metal toothpicks with voice recordings.*"

He wasn't wrong. They *were* creepy, but Amaree hadn't noticed until she was older. As a kid, she was just impressed that she could make little people out of metal. Ansel helped her make the voice boxes with the pre-recorded sentences.

"That's beside the point. I can still make her one," Amaree said as they came to an elevator.

Kava looked down at the button, and it instantly depressed. To her, he said, "I'll let her father know so he can talk to his mate about it."

Amaree couldn't fathom why a Boore family lived on board. But Kava wasn't crazy, so there had to be a perfectly reasonable explanation for it.

The elevator dinged. As they stepped inside, Kava didn't say anything. When the cab stopped at level three, Kava escorted her out, past the medical unit to the second cabin. He tapped in the code for the door and let her in. "When you're done unpacking, my mate and I will go over the plan with you."

Amaree dropped her stuff, not interested in unpacking yet, and walked back out. "I'm more interested in what you have to say."

He didn't reply as he turned around and headed back to the elevator.

The captain's office had an eight-seater Minky table, a floor-to-ceiling Minky screen, and two chillers situated next to a lounge bed covered in a black fur blanket.

Standing at the Minky screen was a female. She flipped through a series of lists that Amaree didn't recognize. The female didn't turn around, and Kava simply pointed to the Minky table. "She'll join us when she's finished. She deep-dives when she's researching."

Amaree nodded, unsure who the female was or what she had to do with the plan to enter the black zone.

"Ah, that's right," Kava said. "You haven't met. That's my mate. Her name is Fenton, and she works for Admiral Rannn. He asked her to retrieve Commander Gammon who supposedly has top-secret information."

Looking back at the female, Amaree remembered her father saying that Kava had gotten mated—her cousin, who didn't usually like anyone besides his family. And even then, he didn't share anything.

Not even his thoughts.

Kava was such a powerful Cerebral, he had been labeled a Master Elder. He could even hide his thoughts from other Cerebrals. His Cerebral title was Kava - The Stone Maker. As in he could literally pull the elements together and make planets if he so desired.

Amaree wondered if Fenton understood the enormity of Kava's abilities.

"Fenton is Penner's daughter," clipped Kava.

"Penner? As in Ansel's brother?"

Her cousin nodded once.

Kava was mated to a Numan. Holy Seth, that was unexpected. Numans were brilliant. Amaree was pleased to know that Kava had mated for intelligence. If Amaree ever married, she too wanted someone brilliant.

Checking once more to see if Fenton were close to being finished, she asked as respectfully as possible, "Is *mating* a term you use instead of married?"

Kava shook his head twice. "I'm a Cerebral, but I'm also a Silk Demon. Fenton's not fully Numan. So, we're mated—the biological way."

Kava was a quarter Terren and a quarter Silk Demon, though he had no Silk thorns. Thorns were mental barbs Silk Demons used to imbed themselves in other people, connecting their minds and allowing the Demon to steal sleep. If Kava was a Demon, Amaree didn't see it. But then again, she didn't understand DNA, so she didn't challenge him.

Well, she didn't outright disagree when she asked, "How do you know that you're Demon side mated? I mean if you think about it, the majority of your genetics are races that marry."

"I don't know how to describe it other than my Demon side is very strong. I have a Silk Demon mind palace and thorns."

"Really?" she asked not believing because throughout their childhood, neither he nor his parents talked about him having those abilities.

Kava smirked, "Want me to prove it?"

Leaning back, "No thanks."

Kava extended his fingers as if he was offering to touch her and implanted a thorn. She pointed at his hand, "Touching me wouldn't prove anything. I don't have the equipment to verify it."

"I don't need to touch you, to implant a Cerebral thorn."

She chuckled. "A Cerebral thorn?" There was no such thing. He was messing with her, like he did when they were kids.

He flicked his fingers, and Amaree got an intense headache that throbbed through her skull. Her eyes closed, and she hissed out a breath.

The pressure and pain were gone a second later. Amaree dropped her hand from her face and calmly but sternly straightened, shooting a glare at her cousin.

"I was implanting a Cerebral thorn in your mind," Kava said, leaning both forearms on the table.

"So, you say," she added dryly.

He looked at her as if he was disappointed. "Can you explain how you have your metal talent? And yet no other Cerebral has that?"

No, she couldn't.

"Can you explain my stone gift or the fact that I have a ten-thousand-mile telepathic range."

No, she couldn't explain his affinity for matter. She also didn't know his range was that extensive. According to the Cerebral medical archives, Kava's father, a Master Elder, had the longest range at five-thousand-miles. An Elder had five hundred. A Functional had fifty miles of tele-range.

More to the point, how long did Kava know this? And why did he keep it a secret? The medical archives would need to be updated.

She sat forward and covered her mouth wondering what else he kept to himself.

Kava hesitated, rubbing his thumb under his fingers. "Those I implant with a Cerebral thorn are bound to me. No matter where they are, I can hear them. I have infinite range."

Infinite range? She didn't know how to process that, but she did remember Ansel saying Kava was the Master of Masters.

"Ree," Kava said, gaining her attention. "There's a lot of things my brothers and I don't talk about, mainly because we don't want anyone to know. But you and I can go over those things later. Right now, I want to explain the mission – and your part in it."

Against her better judgment, she looked at him stupidly, waiting for him to explain.

"Your part of this will be the difference between a successful mission and a failed one with a body count in the six digits."

"I don't understand," she said, wondering what could possibly cause a six figure body count. "Plus, you're a Master Elder with infinite range. You don't need my help." Giving in to a hint of self pity, she added, "Besides, I'm not even classed as a Cerebral. I'm barely one step above Terran."

No one talked about the Cerebral council deciding that she couldn't be classed as anything because she didn't have even basic telepathy range. Meaning, she could call herself a Cerebral hybrid, but she was neither a Functional nor an Elder or Master Elder.

Her lack of telepathy was an obvious flaw, and her telekinesis was limited to what she saw.

It didn't hurt to admit her weakness anymore. Not like it used to.

Kava's voice wasn't exactly soft, like a male trying to tread carefully, but for Kava, it was close enough. "Fenton is brilliant, and even she was caught and enslaved by the pirate queen. She spent weeks in a metal cell, negotiating and working for the queen, desperately trying to get free. When the queen finally let her go, she sent Fenton into a one-way trap."

Amaree could see why Fenton wouldn't want to go back to a place she had been jailed—even if she knew the way in.

"Fenton can't go in and get out on her own. She's smart, but she's not able, like you or me."

At that, Amaree felt her brows rise. Partially in confusion and a bit in offense. Because if he was making a roundabout declaration that she was going into a pirates' ship or whatever, he was a thousand percent wrong. "Which is why you'll be going. You have the most skill."

"The last time I went into the black zone, androids destroyed my ship. The pirate queen knows me and my abilities. She will kill all her prisoners and escape long before I get past the android-controlled ships."

Amaree huffed. "If you can't make it through, then I wouldn't even scratch the surface. Not to mention, it sounds like a death mission, and I'm not suicidal."

Kava folded his arms over his chest and leaned back. "There is nowhere you can go that I won't be with you. I won't let anything happen to you. I promise."

His sincerity conflicted her logic.

"Let me go over the plan with you and give you a chance to understand what I'm asking of you. That way, if you decide not to do it, it won't be because you can't help, it'll be because you won't."

Damn it if that didn't strike her hard. As a doctor, she was expected to help, no matter what. Kava had to know that, and he was using it against her. But also...he was right. She might be able to save someone. And not just in the medical sense, which would be a refreshing change.

Fenton turned around as she grinned, "Got it."

Amaree had no idea what that meant.

"I found a sloop that was used by a traveling doctor," Fenton said, taking a seat next to Kava.

"Why didn't we use mine if you needed a sloop?" Amaree asked.

"Your sloop can be traced back to you. Where you're going, you don't want to bring that kind of attention home with you. We needed to find a ship with the right medical look, without the personal information," Kava answered.

Amaree was equally impressed and deeply concerned. "Where exactly will I be flying this ship?"

"Angny," Fenton said.

"Angny is a planet inside the Federation," Amaree explained to Fenton. To Kava she asked, "I thought you were going to the black zone. The black zone is in the Outworlds."

Kava held up a finger. "As a doctor I know it's natural to ask questions first, but you need to reign that in. Listen to the whole plan, then ask your questions. Okay?"

FIVE
ANGNYS AND THEIR KNIVES

Amaree growled as she kicked the dash console, furious at the hunk of junk sloop. It was no wonder the past owner put it up for sale. "You couldn't hold on for five more seconds?"

The ship had gone dead seconds before she landed, causing the whole massive heap to fall ten feet with a loud crash. Sitting in a hard, metal chair made the landing extra painful, and all she could do was fume at the hunk of junk.

When she stood to gather her wits, she noticed that her neck ached. Unfortunately, all of her medscopes were back on the Maw. Worse, she didn't even have a simple pain-relieving tab to help.

As she looked, she saw that the door was dented, and the ship was lying on its side. Amaree wanted to pick up her Minky pad and tell her cousin that their plan was already failing. Instead of looking like a basic Terran, Amaree would have to use her telekinesis to cut a hole in the ship to escape.

She mentally heated the door hinges and kicked at the flat surface in frustration. It wilted back like a silver petal. The damage looked believable enough for a Terran to have freed herself.

Sliding out the opening and careful not to slice her skin on the sharp edges, she dropped a few feet to the blue landing pad. She scanned the area, looking for what her cousin's mate had called the pirate queen's crew.

The street market was loud, and there were a lot of people, but it in no way looked festive like the markets on Amaree's home moon. Instead, she saw several female Angnys, scowling and tossing items onto tables, back at the female who attempted to sell said items.

The sellers behind the tables were also loud, calling out their products, attempting to catch shoppers' interests.

Most of the tables displayed colorful fruits, deadly-looking vegetables, solid-color clothes, and barbaric weapons.

An older male with saggy grey skin and a maroon and gold tunic stopped in front of Amaree and cast his gaze over the table.

The male noticed that she was watching. He gave her a brief smile in greeting and then lifted his hand and pointed. "I killed my first opponent with that hatchet."

Amaree didn't want to contradict him, but she couldn't help it. "Are you sure it was that one?"

He reached over and picked it up. Handing the weapon to her with the handle in the front, he said, "See the break in the handle?"

She did.

"That was from my tenth fight. I went up against a cyborg. His metal arm turned into a mini canon. I meant to run, but I fell back against a boulder and cracked the handle."

"If you fell, how did you win the fight?"

The male chuckled as he returned the weapon. "I was

fighting doubles. My partner killed the cyborg before he could get me."

"Oh, that's good."

The male reached out and grabbed a small black knife with a purple metallic shine to it. This time when he held it out, he said, "It was good he saved me. He was a good sparring friend. But at the end of the fight, we were told that only one person could leave the arena alive."

Oh.

Amaree felt her soul shrivel. This was why the planet was how it was—the inhabitants were absolutely ruthless.

"This is a Fire Fervor knife. You can tell it's not made by any of the materials from around here because the metal shines purple."

Amaree had read about that race, but they primarily lived on one of the planets that weren't aligned with the Federation, so she never went into that area.

"Do you know what a Fire Fervor is?"

"They're a race of Outworlders who it's believed have living fire in their blood. It's not true, but they do have thick blood that runs hotter than any other race. Their skin is ashy grey. Some have long horns coming out of their heads and fiery hair. Again, it's not that they have fire inside them. It's that some possess a distinct skin chemical that, if rubbed a certain way, catches fire. In the arenas, I assume their natural defense is throwing fireballs."

The old Angny looked her over again, this time with keen eyes. Eyes that looked as if they were reliving an old memory. "That's right. Do you know what's special about Fire Fervor weapons?"

She shrugged. "I have no idea."

The male handed the blade to her. Hesitantly, she took it. The Angny told her, "It can't be melted down. It's like an alloric metal, but it's called frostic. Fire Fervor weapons never dull either, so it's a weapon worth having."

Amaree nodded and went to hand the knife back, but she stopped because she realized something about it was odd. She didn't feel connected to it. She could feel the vibration of all other metals and could easily distance the range, making them pliable. Even alloric, the strongest metal used for spaceship engines and hulls. But the weapon in her hand had no vibration at all.

"I've seen the same look on young gladiators who've found their favorite weapon."

Amaree handed the blade back to the male. "It's a good knife, but I am looking for someone to fix the engine on my ship."

The male didn't take the weapon. Instead, he looked her over and said, "That's a nice beaded necklace. I'll take that for the knife."

Considering that he wasn't the seller, she thought the whole thing was odd. But also, the necklace had been a gift from a Kingling named Moddoe, given to her when she was just a baby. She never took it off. Amaree's father had once told her that, to a Kingling, it was the mark of a warrior—a strong one with a sharp mind. As a kid, she didn't understand what she had done to earn it. As an adult, she rarely thought about it at all...until someone asked about it. She was about to explain to the male that it didn't come off, but instead, she held up her wrist with the wrapped adroiz diamond.

The male looked but didn't comment. She removed it and held up the fine gold and white inlay, waiting to see if he'd take it instead.

With a slight hint of hesitation, the male took the bracelet and nodded in tacit agreement. Once it was in the male's hands, he dropped it onto the table and gave her a nod of approval. "It's a good weapon, and it's been away from battle for too long. Considering you don't have a male beside you, I'm sure you'll use it before the day's out."

She didn't understand his meaning. "I would thank you, but I'm not sure you're being helpful."

At that, he chuckled and said something just as Kava accessed her mind. *"Get back to the ship. The queen's collector is there looking at it. Tell the gladiator thank you and leave."*

"Thank you," she said to the male and then turned on her heel, immediately starting to run. As she did, she pushed the knife up her shirt. Connecting to the object as a whole, she moved it with her telekinesis until the blade was up on her back. There, she hoped to keep it hidden if she could.

Although it would take constant pressure by her mind.

Back at the landing docks, she saw an older Terran looking at her ship. He had shaggy hair and a thick, wiry, brown-and-grey beard. Peering at her as she walked up, he asked, "Is this your vessel?"

"Yes."

He gave her a look. "Looks kind of banged-up. Does it fly?"

"Not at the moment. But I'm working on finding an engine and someone to install it."

The male slapped the air. "Nah, you don't want to mess with those brothers. They're crooks."

"So I've been told." She flat-out lied, hoping it was the right thing to say.

Concerned, the male asked, "Does that mean you made a deal with them?"

"No, I didn't make any deals."

Visibly relieved, the male touched his chest. "Good. Then you can make one with me. I'm Pandal, the most reliable cargo captain in all the 'verses," the male said, puffing out his chest.

"I'm Amaree," she said, just as Kava said, "*Don't tell him your name.*"

Oops.

"Oh, that's a beautiful name."

"Thank you. But you were saying that you have an engine for sale?"

"Nope," he said, smiling, the cheeks on his round face reddening. "I buy broken ships."

Oh. That's not what she'd expected. "Mine won't be broken for long."

He reached over and patted the hull. "Darlin', this lady isn't moving on her own ever again."

Technically, he was right; and she couldn't find a good counter argument.

"I can see by the look on your face that you know it, too."

In her mind, she asked Kava, "*He's not a telepath, right?*"

"*No, but your expressions are easy to read,*" Kava answered.

"Okay, I can see you're thinking about it. So, why don't I show you what I can offer you in exchange, and you can see if this old girl is worth fixing or if you are interested in buying a new ship," said Pandal.

She scanned the landing pads. "Which ones are yours?"

Chuckling, he said, "I have too many to display here. I'll take you to them and promise you six thousand for this one upfront. So, if you find something of equal value in my stock, then it will be an even trade."

That sounded like a good deal.

Kava's telepathic voice cut into her mind. "*He's a pirate. He doesn't have any ships, Ree. He's lying to you.*"

"Really?" she said aloud, responding to Kava. If that were true, then the Terran was a good liar because he'd convinced even her.

Thankfully, the pirate thought she was talking to him. "I'm

an honest scrapper. I like taking in broken things and fixing them up. I'm one of the few who can say that I love what I do. And I make enough to keep doing it."

Good Seth of Stars, he was good.

"Okay, I can see you like my offer. Is the price too low?"

"No," she said firmly. "The price is great. I would sell it to you right now but..."

"But what?" he asked, leaning forward as if more worried about her than her ship.

"I'm not supposed to sell it. I need to get it fixed so I can..." Clearing her throat, she thought about telling him the truth, but told the lie Fenton had provided instead. "I'm a traveling doctor. I need to be able to get to my next contract."

"Amaree? Are you insane? Stop selling it. He's already planning to kidnap you. Now you're making yourself a mark. Mother of Seth...stop talking," Kava hissed.

Oops.

The pirate nodded as if he understood. "That makes sense. Of course, you would need a working ship."

"I really do," she said nervously, wondering how bad it was that he now knew she was a doctor.

"Very bad, but I'm going to take care of it," her cousin answered. *"Just don't tell anyone else."*

"Well," said Pandal, pressing his hand to his chest. "I just so happen to have a little sloop in my cargo bay. The guy who was going to buy it backed out. If you like it, you can sign over the ship's title, and you can get back to the job of helping the sick."

"Okay. Yeah. That works," she said, a little more nervous now, knowing what was supposed to happen.

The male smiled warmly. "It's a done deal. Let's head over to my ship."

The Terran's vessel was not a Federation ship but was uniquely shaped. It had spikes on the top and two parallel S-shaped wings. Stepping up the ramp, she asked, "Did you build this ship?"

"Nope. Found it. One of my many talents."

"Oh. Really? This is an Outworlder ship, right?" she asked, stepping into the ship's cargo bay. It was full of boxes, and a bunch of crew members were moving them around and hollering. She didn't see a single ship, just people in tubes of various sizes, in different states of emotions. Some were screaming, others were crying, and a few were unmoving as if trying to ignore what was happening to them.

"You look confused," said the male from behind her. "Is this your first time on a slave ship?"

She turned around to see a phaser pointed at her face. The fake-friendly pirate looked at her with beady, black eyes. "Now, be a good doctor and walk to your tube. You know what a shot to the gut will do, and I'm sure you want to skip the suffering part of the process."

Amaree closed her mouth and let him direct her. She knew this was all part of the plan, but she didn't expect to feel actual betrayal from the person she had known was lying to her. But she had never been in a situation like this before, either.

SIX
WHY AM I SAVING A CANNIBAL?

Amaree was still in the tube, but at least she was in the holding area of the asteroid city. Kava had told her that the pirate queen was on her way. The anticipation of seeing a new race drummed inside Amaree.

"*She's not that impressive,*" Kava said. "*If her race was that great, she wouldn't be the last of them.*"

That didn't help to sway Amaree's interest at all. In fact, it made it worse. What's happened to the queen's race? Why did they all die?

"*Mostly because they glow. From what Fenton has researched, her race was taken and sold as gifts.*"

Amaree was sure that Kava didn't want her to feel sorry for the female, but he made it hard not to.

A spark of light in her peripheral vision caught Amaree's attention. Turning her head to the left, she realized that it was a person. Fenton had told her that the pirate queen was a Yuorn—a race of people that generated light.

Knowing what to expect and seeing it were two vastly different things.

The pirate queen looked like a model from the Sennite

fashion magazines. She was tall with curves, the heels of her thin shoes perfectly matching the tight dress she wore. Her hair was long, curled, and dripping with what looked like golden diamonds.

When the female stopped in front of her tube, Amaree had to freeze her face to keep from smiling. The queen pointed at Amaree's tube. "Open this one."

A Hetten male moved forward without hesitation and opened the tube. The pirate queen pursed her lips and tilted her head. "I am told you're a doctor. But looking at you, you look too young to be a well-established healer."

Amaree didn't know if she was supposed to sell her skills or not.

"*Not. Absolutely do not oversell yourself. We need her to forget you after this is all over,*" Kava said urgently.

"Well?" the queen said.

Amaree shrugged.

"You are a doctor? Aren't you?"

Amaree nodded.

"Are you any good at extracting gramones from Graches?"

Was she any good at what? Doctors didn't remove the hormones because it was necessary for the Grachs' health. The only type of doctors who did that were the ones on Verrain, the cyborg planet. They were more about enhancing the body. "Are you asking if I know how to remove the lipids? Or take a sample for testing?"

The queen chuckled. The five males behind her laughed, too. "I guess that answers that question."

Amaree had no idea what question had been answered.

"My man here will take you to one of my prisoners. You will remove all the gramones from his dead body and give them to me."

Amaree couldn't think of a single ethical reason for the

queen to harvest gramones. It eluded to the female's sick perversion and maliciousness.

"You know, I don't like talkative females. They're annoying and never have anything interesting to say. But I also don't like quiet ones. They always seem to be up to something." The queen's luminescence grew, and Amaree felt the heat and had to close her eyes at the brightness. "If you're hiding something, I will find out and make your life here a living hell."

"I'm not hiding anything."

"You're thinking something," the queen persisted.

"I was thinking I wish I wasn't here and wondering how long it will take for someone to notice I'm missing."

The queen laughed again, this time with a big smile. When she finished, she dabbed her eye. "I like you. You're honest, even if you shouldn't be." To the Hetten, she said, "Take her to the cannibal. When she's done, bring her back to me."

"Cannibal?" Amaree's mind spun wildly at the inhuman and dishonorable practice.

The queen's eyes sparkled with amusement. "Here In the Outworlds, not all beasts have fur and feathers."

Amaree knew that people could be monsters, but a cannibal was next level.

The queen gave a scathing look to the Hetten who then pulled out a phaser and pointed to the door. "Walk."

She did so, quietly. Outside the holding room, the walls narrowed to where two people couldn't even walk side by side. The guard led her down another hall and five flights of stairs, then into a dank-smelling asteroid cell with metal doors.

At the end of the hall, the male used a manual thumb lock and pushed her in. "You stay here while I get the supplies."

"You're going to leave me in a cell with a dead person?" she said, trying to keep from stepping into the room, the smell of death stinging her nostrils.

"The thing inside there should have died multiple times. Each time, he ends up waking up. So, no, I'm not going in there."

Amaree didn't want to sound patronizing, but once a person was dead, they were dead.

The Hetten took her arm and pushed her farther into the dark room. The light from the hall gave her insight into where the smell was coming from. A rotting carcass lay off to the side. Another lump of a body was curled in the corner, surrounded by a dark puddle of something—either blood or vomit, going by the acidic smell.

Covering her mouth, Amaree didn't want to think about the bacteria currently covering every inch of the room. Lost in her thoughts, she didn't act fast enough to catch the guard unawares when he shut her in. The light left, but the memory of what she'd seen stayed.

Pulling up her shirt to cover her nose and mouth, she tried not to breathe. Backing up, she hit the wall but then leaned forward, not wanting to touch anything. She had seen a lot of things during her medical career. Had been in some pretty bad situations...though nothing compared to what she was in now.

"Hell apparently has no bounds," grated a male voice.

Immediately, Amaree's stomach dropped. He was *alive?* The cannibal was alive? Oh, Seth, no.

"Be careful, Ree. I can't see him through your eyes, so I can't defend you until he touches you or a light turns on."

Darkness was a weakness that all Cerebrals had. They couldn't mentally connect with something they couldn't see. Leaning closer, Amaree held still as she mentally removed the knife from her back and held it close by so she could use it to kill whoever attacked her—if they did.

Kava's sudden voice made her jump. *"Fenton got a hold of the Silk Demon. She says the commander is in a cell and is sick."*

"Not right now," Amaree whispered in her mind. *"Dealing with a cannibal at the moment."*

"I know. I just wanted you to know that the commander is still alive, and you can't get caught using your abilities. So, put away the knife. The queen has video feeds from every cell, and they can see in the dark."

Damn it.

Against all her instincts, she replaced the knife.

"You smell like a female, but there is also a hint of ozone. Are you a cyborg? It would make sense the queen sent in a cyborg, knowing I don't eat metal."

Oh. My. Seth. How a person could smell anything other than death in here was beyond Amaree. He must have seen her come in.

She didn't want the foul air in her lungs, but she had to respond. "The queen sent me in here to extract your gramones. But she said you were dead."

There was a hollow grunt. "Not yet. But she came close with a vaporized annaphellix bomb."

Amaree felt her face scrunch. "There is no way you lived through being exposed to vaporized annaphellix. It causes anaphylactic shock."

"Believe it or not. Regardless, I'm still alive. So, there you have it."

"It couldn't have been annaphellix, then."

"I know annaphellix when I smell it."

Oh, really? "You're saying you've been exposed to it repeatedly?"

"No, just once. But I recognized the scent."

"I understand that you believe that, but I'm a medical doctor. Trust me when I say that no one can live through that."

"And hell just keeps twisting the knife."

"I have no idea what that means," she said, knowing very

well that she should have kept quiet. Cannibals were known to have mental issues, and this guy was clearly mental.

"Let's just say I'm not picky about the food I eat, so long as I eat. As a male, I am inclined to keep you alive. Even I have standards for who I'll eat. But, to be honest, you being a doctor with an irritating know-it-all-attitude makes the lines I'm willing to cross kind of blurry."

"I can shut up," she said, hoping that appeased him.

"That's probably a good idea."

The cell fell into silence. With every second that ticked by, Amaree waited for something, anything to indicate that the cannibal was moving towards her.

"You're some kind of hybrid, aren't you?"

What happened to keeping quiet? Oh, yeah, she was in a room with a mentally unstable cannibal. "Yeah. Terran and Kooyan," she said, figuring he'd want to know. She'd stopped telling people that she was a Cerebral because they tended to fear her reading their minds.

"I never met a Kooyan before. That must be the extra spice I smell."

Amaree disregarded that last bit because there was no way he could tell that she was a hybrid by her scent. No race's sense of smell was that good—or at least any of the races she knew about.

There might be a race in the wilds of the Outworlds, but she didn't know about it. Then again, the male could be a hybrid, too.

"What's your name?" he asked.

"Amaree."

"*Good Seth of Stars, you don't listen, do you?*" Kava said with a heavy dose of frustration.

"How long have you been the queen's slave pirate?"

"Counting the ten-minute conversation with the queen

before this, I'd say roughly thirty minutes." She heard a noise that could have been a half-laugh or a chuff.

"So, you're not a loyal slave?"

"No."

"But you're a pirate."

"I'm a doctor, actually."

Kava cursed in her head, and she almost smiled. The cannibal wasn't more of a threat after learning her name.

"And how did you end up here?"

"A consecutive series of poor choices," she said honestly.

He grunted. "For someone who's fallen this far, you don't seem to emit the right sense of fear or self-hatred. But that could be because, like you said, you're an idiot."

"That's not what I said," she clipped out.

"I summarized."

Wow. Just...wow. A cannibal with the nerve to call her an idiot. At least, she didn't eat people.

"Then again, since you're so inclined, there *is* another poor choice you can make. And it might not end in being stuck here forever."

"Oh, really? And what is that?"

He was silent for a good long moment. She worried that she had insulted him and that he would go back to thinking about eating her. But she heard the first breath of, "Get the guard to focus on you." Said from right next to her.

Amaree screamed as she jerked away from the cannibal. The loud and reverberating pop of the door being warped back was a sound she knew well. She grabbed the knife and waited to see if the cannibal would touch her. If so, she would defend herself.

"There's that ozone scent again. What are you up to, sneaky hybrid?" The male had moved again. This time, he was speaking from somewhere above her. Not as close as last time, but too close for comfort.

"Just catching my breath. You scared me."

"That was the point. You're supposed to be scared. When the guard comes back, you need to be scared. And the acting isn't enough. You need to really feel it."

"I feel it."

"No, you don't. Not while you have a weapon."

There was no way he knew that unless he could see in the dark.

He sniffed the air. "Frostic? Now that's not a normal weapon for a doctor."

She had no idea how he knew that. Tightening her hold on dagger's hilt, just in case she needed to...*discourage* the cannibal from trying to hurt her. "Doctor's don't have weapons. We have tools."

"Tools are weapons. The only difference is the application."

That was the most irritatingly truthful thing she'd ever heard. Worse, she couldn't think of a good comeback. "Well... maybe for you."

"Are you saying that you won't use that *tool* if I attack you?" he asked, moving closer to the floor. She could tell by the sound of his voice as it descended.

Moving the knife so she pointed it in his direction, she said, "Of course, I would. All people have a survival instinct."

"So you say. How about you prove it?"

She held her breath, waiting for him to attack.

"When the guard comes back in, you're gonna distract him by luring him farther inside. Then, I'm going to kill him. We'll be free, and you can follow me and increase your chances of escape. That is if you can keep up."

She didn't relax her grip on the knife, but she did inhale as she thought about his plan. It was decent and would get her out of this rancid, rotting cell so she could find the commander she had been tasked to retrieve. But it was eerie to hear him speak so clearly. As if he weren't an addle-minded cannibal.

"You don't smell relieved. I find that telling," he said in an amused voice.

"Graches don't have superior olfactory structures. And even if you have a cybernetic upgrade, the death permeating this space is too strong to smell anything else."

He chuckled, "Is that right?"

She didn't answer because he knew she was—he just didn't want to admit it.

Something slid from in front of her to her left. She moved the knife to follow the sound and was pleased when the male's voice came from a new spot. "You know what I'm wondering? I'm wondering why you're really here. Was it because you were caught or because you wanted to be? Because I can't imagine any of the queen's pets not checking you for weapons."

Damn. Why were all the crazy ones so damn smart? Again, she kept quiet.

"You know," he said amusedly, "the more you stay quiet, the more I learn."

"That's not a real thing," she heard herself say.

He chuckled. "I can prove it."

"I doubt it, but I'm ready to hear you out," she said, genuinely interested in his crazy mental process.

Without warning, she heard the sliding sound of someone unlocking the door. Moving forward to get out of the way, a hand grabbed her arm, lifted her up, and turned her towards the door as it opened. She quickly moved the knife to her thigh and used her abilities to keep it there, out of sight.

The same guard that'd brought her in reached out and handed her something wrapped in a medical-grade sealant. "Here, get the stuff."

"It's pitch-dark in here," she said, backing farther into the room. "How the hell am I supposed to get any of the gramones without being able to see?"

"Not my problem. You're a doctor, figure it out." The male stepped in and pushed the stuff he held into her chest. "Take it."

"It's not even in sanitized bags." She held her arms up, just as the cannibal's hand reached out from behind the door and pulled the guard in. The male yelped before she heard a pop. Amaree closed her eyes, not liking the sound of death.

The body flopped to the floor. The top half was visible, and she saw that his head was turned at an unnatural angle.

"Well, at least you're really a doctor," the cannibal said.

She shook her head, upset that she was conflicted over the death of a pirate. This was real life, and it was expected that some might have to die. But seeing how easily a life could be taken was not something she enjoyed.

"I can't follow you, but I hope you get free. I need to find someone first."

"Figured that. Family member or husband?" he asked, still in the shadows as if he was hiding his identity.

But then she remembered that Donnies—the cannibal pirates from the Federation side of space—were known to be malformed with congenital disorders. The male was obviously hiding his hideousness.

It was the first human reaction he showed and if he wasn't a cannibal and killer she might be flattered. "Neither. The Federation lost an important person. I'm here to find them," she answered as she stepped into the hall. Looking both ways, she saw no one. Taking the knife in hand, she retreated to the left. She suspected that the male would leave when he was ready, but something made her turn around to see what he looked like. She had to know.

The male stepped out. He had Grach-like brown skin, dark

hair, and eyes. His face was weathered, and bruises marred his jaw. One eye looked as if a blood vessel had popped in it, and his cheeks were sallow. Nothing about his base features exhibited a disorder.

His shirt was filthy, which seemed appropriate for where he had been jailed, but she would know the black Federation uniform anywhere. Even if she didn't, his pants and Federation-issued boots were more than enough to confirm that the cannibal had once been Federation-employed.

Or he ate one and stole his clothes.

"What's your captive's name?" he asked in a tone she had not heard before.

She wasn't that stupid...

"*Tell him,*" Kava instructed.

That didn't sound smart, but it wasn't her plan. "Commander Gammon," she answered. "Do you know where he is?"

The cannibal-Grach-possible-hybrid closed his eyes and cleared his throat as if hearing the name had cut him deeply. Whatever he felt, he got over it fast. "Yeah, I know him."

Trotting over, he didn't say anything, just looked at her and then her knife before holding out his hand.

Was he going to help her rescue him? That was unexpected. "Are you going to give it back?" she asked.

"Sure, as long as you don't mind all the blood."

She didn't like the mental image of what he planned to do, but she handed it over anyway. "You can always wash it off before you give it back."

Rolling his eyes, he wrapped his hand around the hilt and mumbled, "Sure, hun. I'll sanitize it too while I'm at it." He peered both ways at the intersection and used his chin to tell her which way he was headed. Following him, she watched as he scanned each hall. Once they arrived at the stairs, he looked back and whispered, "There is a ninety-nine percent chance we will be seen and shot at. Unless they shoot you dead, keep following me."

"That doesn't sound like a good plan. And I've heard some bad ones before."

He snickered. "Like the plan to get kidnapped by pirates to come and get me?"

Me?

Oh. OH!

This was Gammon? His Federation picture looked a lot better. It was most likely caused by the drastic change in his diet. But more to the point, they were talking about his horrible plan. "Yeah, your plan is worse."

The male's brows pulled together as if he weren't sure whether she was telling the truth or not. She didn't care if he believed her. And she didn't clarify anything, either.

"At least with my plan, you have a chance to live."

Did he not hear himself? "You just said to keep running unless they shoot me dead."

"Yeah, exactly," he said smartly as if making perfect sense—which he wasn't. Not at all.

Cannibals.

They jogged up the stairs and cracked the second-story door. Peeking out, she saw a slew of ships parked in the docking bay, and thousands of folks moving about, most yelling. It was loud, and she was awestruck at the immensity of it.

Gammon shut the door and looked at her as if he were pissed. "They picked a winner with you, didn't they?"

"First of all, why are you being so rude? If I wasn't here, you would still be in that cell. Secondly, why are you calling me a winner as if I did something wrong?"

He moved closer, and she realized that the foul smell of death was coming from him. It smelled acidic and oily. His breath, amazingly enough, wasn't as awful as the rest of him.

Maybe his Grach scent wasn't the smell of death. Perhaps the foulness simply permeated his clothes. Either way, she leaned back, unable to be that close.

Gammon closed the gap and glared at her, making her knees lock. "You want to know why I'm pissed? Because someone out there in the Federation wants me dead. And whoever it is, found a way to set up a mission that was guaranteed to fail. You are the last person who should be here. You're so green, you could sprout flowers. Whoever set this whole thing up, did it knowing you would die. That means, either you were just a random nobody, or the bastard specifically wanted you dead. Either way, this whole thing is screwed, and when we get free, we won't just have the Federation bastards gunning for us, we'll also have the pirate queen's minions scouring every inch of space, looking for us. And they will never quit. So, yeah, I'm pissed."

Straightening her back, Amaree said, "Being pissed won't help us get out. Focus on what we need to do next and keep the end goal in mind."

He held her eyes for a moment too long. Long enough for her to wonder if he was concerned about something else and not telling her about it. "What?"

Gammon looked away and then back at her as if he weren't sure what to say—or maybe he didn't want to say it.

Wait. Was he worried they wouldn't make it? Did he know his plan was stupid?

"Look," she started, but he cut her off by opening the door.

Grabbing her hand, he pushed it to his lower back. "Hold on to my belt loop, and let's hope Fenock of Fortune is being generous."

Amaree grabbed the loop at the back of his pants, wondering why a Grach—even a hybrid—was talking about Fenock.

As they left the safety of the stairwell, her heart pumped harder. She knew that if she looked scared, she would draw more attention, so she tried to calm her nerves. It wasn't that far to the ships. She could do this.

"The hell?" a male yelled with a finger pointing directly at her. Turning to the others, the male shouted, "The cannibal's loose! Look, right there! Bastard ate my friend's fingers."

Gammon growled, one that was deep and animalistic, followed by a fluttered breath. In no way was that sound normal.

Gammon threw Amaree's knife, and it landed dead center in someone's chest. He rushed forward, breaking her hold on his belt. Gammon took the blade, grabbed the closest pirate's face, opened his mouth, and bit off a chunk of the male's cheek.

Shocked, Amaree's mouth dropped open. Who did that?

Gammon took off as if he were going to attack someone else but then whipped his head back as if he knew she wasn't behind him.

His mouth, chin, and neck were splattered with blood. He growled again, but it was a different, deeper rumble, as if he weren't threatening her life. But the thick finger pointed down at his side was anything but subtle. The male was an absolute savage, and she was at a loss for how to respond to someone so primitive.

Letting someone like him loose was dangerous. Obeying his barbaric commands made her feel simpleminded.

Three males rushed at Gammon and attacked with knives and a phaser. Emotionally and physically frozen at the barbarity in all four males, she remained still, not wanting to take part. Blood sprayed, and she felt her heart lurch when one of the attackers died—horribly.

Gammon spit out a chunk of flesh, and she felt sick.

Without warning, a hand wrapped around her waist and

her mouth. Fingers dug into her face, and a male voice said in her ear, "You're a pretty thing. I'll enjoy you a lot more than my current bed partner."

Shock made Amaree slow to react. She was still trying to come to terms with what was happening to her and what the male had said. But before she had time to do anything, a deathly growl reverberated next to her. Without having to look, she knew who it was. And that the male who'd let her go was probably dead—his scream was a good indication.

Gammon grabbed her arm and pulled her to a run. They didn't get far before another group of men came at them, and Gammon pushed her forward. "Keep going."

In her head, she yelled, "*Kava, I need to use my ability.*"

Immediately, he responded, "*Not yet. Gammon's a fighter. He's fine. Keep running.*"

Gammon wasn't a fighter...he was an animal.

She turned back after finding a spot with an open area free of people and watched Gammon slice someone's throat open while kicking someone else who was trying to crawl away. A large Krant ran up with a huge-looking club with spikes. She reached out mentally to stop the attacker.

A millisecond later, Gammon took the knife and threw it directly at the Krant. The blade slid right into his eye. Blood sprayed, and those around him screamed. The massive yellow body was like a large tree, falling to the ground and landing with a bounce.

Amaree gasped, letting go of him mentally. Her stomach twisted with nausea. She couldn't deal with all the death.

Gammon strutted over, removed the knife from the male's eye, and then peered over at her. She had never been so utterly transfixed and disgusted in her life. The cannibal just shook his head.

Scanning the area, he jogged to her, grabbed her by the

wrist, and pulled her towards the ships, ignoring the chorus of screams and gunshots.

Gammon veered to a galleon ship, and Kava yelled in her head, "*Not that one. It's broken.*"

"Not that one," she said aloud. "It's broken."

"*The black one with the blue tips,*" Kava instructed.

"The black one with the blue tips," she called out, having no idea where that ship was. Gammon immediately changed directions, just as a group of people from behind a transporter jumped out. Two males and a female went after Gammon, all armed with phasers. Another male came after her, but before he could touch her, she held him off with her ability, then reached out and grabbed his shirt, yanking him down face-first. With her controlling every movement, he landed hard. His nose was broken for sure, but he'd live.

Gammon had already ripped into the two males who were wriggling on the floor. When the female shot at him again, he jumped, grabbed her by the face, and threw her against the ship. Gammon looked at her, then the male beside her.

Amareee didn't see even a flicker of pride in his eyes. Instead, he almost looked upset. As if he didn't like that she'd defended herself. Or maybe it was because up until then, she hadn't done a very good job of fighting. What if he thought she was being lazy?

Gammon grabbed her wrist again and pulled her into a run once more. Now that they were past the transporter, she could see a blue sloop with blue tips, but it had a bigger tail and definitely a faster engine.

Behind them, she heard an eruption of screams and phaser shots. She wanted to turn around, but Gammon was running too fast. If she pivoted, she would likely trip and fall.

The sloop's ramp started to lower, and a Night Demon in a pair of boxers walked down the ramp, his movements stiff. His expression was furious, as if something or someone had seriously pissed him off. Gammon ran right past, and the Demon didn't even turn around. She did hear him say, "I should have asked for five million. My ship is worth it."

Amaree didn't have to guess who he'd talked to.

Inside the ship, Gammon hit the recall ramp button and then kept running through the small cargo area into the hall. He didn't let her go until they were both on the bridge. It was a two-seater, and Gammon pushed her into the navigation seat.

He powered up the ship and brought up the navigation screen. With a free hand, he grabbed the knife from his belt, wiped off both sides of the blade on his pants, and handed it back to her. "As promised," he said.

Amaree took the dagger with two fingers and pressed it to the side of the chair where she mentally molded some of the chair to create a sheath.

Gammon grabbed the controls with a snicker. "When we get out of this, you have a lot of explaining to do."

The ship was in the air in minutes, and Gammon pushed the engines hard. The first set of docking bay doors were closing. "Find the torpedoes on the ship's log and fire them at the second set of doors. I can get us past the first ones, but we need a way out, or we aren't getting out of here."

Amaree took a deep breath. Now that they were escaping, this part of Kava's plan was *her* responsibility. Shooting the door was not part of the scheme, but she didn't really have the time to explain it to Gammon. Reaching out with her mind, she connected to the exterior doors.

"Damn it, you can't follow orders for nothing," yelled Gammon as he tried to reach over to fire the torpedoes.

"Stop. Just keep flying towards the door," she told him, not taking her eyes from her metal target. She couldn't break her concentration or the connection.

"Not happenin', hun. That's called crashing, and crashing won't solve our problems."

Before he could take over, the lights in the docking bay winked out. The emergency booster lights didn't come on inside the asteroid city, either.

Amaree was sure that was her cousin's doing.

The navigation screen had instantly switched to dark mode so she could see. Gammon pulled away from the throttle. "What the hell? Did you do that?"

She pointed forward. "Keep flying towards the door and trust me."

Gammon reached over to hit the torpedoes again, and she slapped his hand away. "If you can't do it, I will take over," she threatened.

"We can't magically go through the door."

Straining her telekinesis, she mentally grabbed the thrusters and pushed them forward. Gammon tried to pull back, but his physical power was nothing compared to her mental strength.

"Damn it. You're crazy, we are not—" he shouted as the ship passed through liquid metal. Amaree touched the screen to the back view and zoomed in to fix what she could. Once it was sealed, she reselected the front view.

She could feel Gammon's eyes on her, but she didn't feel inclined to explain. There was still one more part to the plan.

"Okay..." he said slowly. "I'm impressed. Confused as hell, but impressed."

Alternatively, she wasn't at all impressed with him.

The navigation screen pinged red with incoming ships. She tapped the screen to widen the view and did a full three-sixty watch. Feeling much more in control and comfortable, she wanted to take over. Using her abilities, she flicked her fingers and floated Gammon from his seat. Moving into the pilot's seat, she grabbed the controls and did what she was good at.

Pushing the ship forward, she smiled as the ship's dexterity was better than hers. On the navigation screen, a series of red dots were closing in fast. She slid her finger across the screen and spread her fingers to enlarge. The first set of ships was all different. She was too far away to use her ability, but the gap was closing fast.

"Let me help," Gammon said from behind her where she still held him in place.

"I'm good," she said in her best doctor's voice.

"I'm a commander for the Federation. I am more than qualified to help you."

"I know who you are, I read your file. But this won't take long."

"The queen controls the entire south portion of the Outworlds. This won't be quick."

Amaree knew it was big, but she had no doubt in this part of the plan. This was what she knew. It was all about keeping calm, reacting fast, and being precise.

The screen flickered, and a second later, a voice call blinked. Without touching the screen, it answered by itself. Amaree didn't understand how that had happened, but maybe it was another thing Kava did. Or perhaps it was Fenton.

Fenton's voice was upbeat when she said, "Ready to melt some ships, my ferrokinesis witch?"

"Already on that," Amaree said as another group of ships shot at her. Cutting to the left, she dropped some flares. Hitting the controls, she got a good look at the nearest ship, mentally found the sensors, and broke them.

"If it's easier to take out the sensors, continue what you're doing. But just know no one is in those ships. They're androids."

Androids? Like the ones that took out Kava?

"There is no such technology," Gammon said from behind her.

"There is. And if you're piloting, be careful of the ships willing to ram you."

"I'm flying," Amaree said and then belatedly added, "Gammon's behind me."

"Floating behind you," Gammon corrected.

Fenton chuckled. "What's with your family and using people as balloons?"

Amaree didn't have time to laugh at the correlation. But she did take hold of the next ship and rip open its engine. It exploded, rocking her and the surrounding vessels.

Fenton harrumphed. "Okay, that works, I guess."

Amaree took another dive and swerved. A handful of ships followed. All unleashed an artillery horde of torpedoes, and there were too many to destroy them all individually. Amaree pulled them to a center point in hopes they blew each other up.

It worked, but the explosion shook her ship.

"You good?" Fenton asked.

"Fine," she said, returning to take down the other spacecraft but without making their engines explode. One by one, she ripped open the bridges and destroyed their systems.

By the tenth one, she was starting to feel a strain in her eyes.

Licking her lips, she bared down and worked her way through the ships and torpedoes still firing on her. She knew she didn't have to fight all the ships; she just had to hold out long enough for Fenton to hack in and power off the android ships.

It was a constant go-go-go, and Amaree was zoned in.

"Oh...no. Brace!" Fenton yelled just as something hit the sloop.

Amaree flew into the controls, and the whole ship felt as if it had been hit by a planet-sized hammer. The ship was in a nosedive when she sat back and pulled back on the controls. The navigation screen flickered, and she knew the sloop was now on reserve power.

Damn.

Gammon moved to the navigation seat. He tapped the Minky screen and moved it in front of her, then opened the same image that was on the navigation screen. He reduced Fenton's call and wordlessly flipped on the torpedoes and flares. Zooming in on the recent attacker who was now beneath her, Gammon shot a set of torpedoes directly at the ship.

Then, he moved his attention to those around them.

Amaree's head throbbed, and she could tell her mental ability was getting weak. But she had no plans to stop. To her surprise, Gammon was able to zero in on each ship for her. There was no tap, zoom, and go.

It was fluid and flawless as they worked together in absolute silence. Several more ships tried to cage them, both from above and below. Gammon took care of them.

Once they were out of that armada, she heard Fenton rattle off a series of coordinates, and Gammon typed them in. Amaree followed the flight path that Gammon had made for her. A bright red ship waited in front of an asteroid belt, the receiving dock door open.

Gammon sat back. His voice was hoarse as he said, "The Maw."

She didn't know why he sounded so upset. Peering over, she asked, "You know my cousin's ship?"

He cut his eyes at her, seeming even more upset. "The ship he attacked and cut everyone's head off? My friend was on it."

That didn't sound like Kava.

"The Federation didn't hire you, did they?" he asked.

"Not me, no," she said, pulling into the docking bay. Once they were down and safely in the ship, she powered down and stood up. Unable to relax...no, she would be unable to think about anything until she was washed and cleaned and back on *her* ship.

"What does Kava want with me?" Gammon asked.

"Nothing. His mate took the job," she said, following the hall to the small cargo bay. Once she was there, she hit the ramp button and stared straight ahead, feeling flushed and mentally *off*.

Gammon stood by the ramp as it descended. He was holding his lower gut area, and the medical professional in her narrowed her eyes.

Blood.

Flowing blood.

Just like before, she mentally switched from distracted to laser-focused and went into doctor-mode. Cursing herself, she added, "I'm such an idiot." Of course, he got hurt. Picking him up with her mind, she turned him flat and then ran through the cargo bay to the elevator. Inside, Gammon said, "Put me down. I'm not that hurt."

"Shut up," she snapped as she ripped off his shirt to see a torso full of bullet holes and cuts.

With a ding, the doors opened, and she took Gammon across the hall to the medical bay. She placed him on the long, white medbed.

"Calm down, I have been in worse shape," he said as she grabbed a drawer and opened it. It was full of napkins. She opened the next one and found it full of tongue depressors.

"What the hell? That's not even where these things go." Opening and shutting more and more drawers, she was losing hope. "Where are the damn medical supplies?" she yelled, pulling out the sanitation wipes and cleaning gel.

The next drawer was full of needles. She needed clamps or tweezers, damn it. Holding up her hand, she cursed. "Fine, I'll do it myself."

She rushed to the sink, washed, rinsed, sanitized, then washed and rinsed again. Then she moved back to Gammon, who was now sitting up. Reaching out to him mentally, she tried to push him down, but nothing happened.

Looking at him as if he were magical, she asked, "How did you do that?"

"Sit up?" he asked sarcastically.

"You need to lay down so I can get the bullets out."

He nodded. "You're right, they do need to come out, but not by you. You're about to drop."

"I'm fine."

"Are you?" he said as if he were playing with her. "Because from where I'm at, it looks like you're having an adrenaline dump."

"I don't have the shakes, and I'm perfectly fine," she said seriously. "I'm fine. Please, lie down, Commander."

"Commander?" he repeated. "Yep, you're crashing."

She pointed to him and hissed. No words...just hissed.

Gammon's lips were pressed into a small smile as he leaned forward and growled. A new growl. A soft one that vibrated and ended in a flutter.

Her stomach in knots over the time wasted and how much blood he was losing, she hissed again. This time longer. She blew as much air through her teeth as she could and shook her head.

Gammon made a new sound, a little whir in his throat. She looked around for something to threaten him with but, miraculously, he lay back down. Not wasting any more time, Amaree lowered the bed with her foot controls and immediately leaned over, reaching for the scanner. And then it dawned on her. Why didn't she scan him first?

That was Medical Triage 101.

How the hell had she forgotten? Standing back, she didn't want to admit that something was wrong. That she wasn't good.

The scan came back with even more wounds than she had

suspected. Thankfully, only two bullets were still inside him. She pushed the scans to the side so she could keep watch on everything that was wrong, and all the blood flowing out of him in small streams.

She grabbed a scalpel and tried to re-mold it, but it didn't work. Refusing to let it go, she pulled one side down and did it manually, like she used to when she was a girl. Metal had always succumbed to her. Obeyed her like clay.

Once the scalpel was tweezers, she reached over, touched his cold skin, and dropped the ends in, grabbing a bullet fragment. She pulled it out slowly, slower than she ever remembered, but she needed to be thorough. If she left any inside him, it would be bad, especially while in the medbed.

Moving to the next wound, she heard Gammon whisper. "They really did find a winner in you."

"I'm saving your life right now. Don't be rude to your doctor."

"I wasn't," he said softly, and that made her stop.

She looked over his face. His eyes were closed and he had a smile on his lips. He looked at ease, which was odd because he should have been numb...oh, crap.

She hadn't numbed the wounds.

Letting her head fall back, she wanted to smack herself, but then she would have to rewash. Getting her head in the game, she pulled the last sliver from the wound and then turned around, pulling up the procedures for the medbed just to be sure she hadn't forgotten anything else.

Scanning, she could barely see the wounds, but she was sure that she was reading them right. Nodding quickly, she felt confident that he was good to go.

Turning around, she saw that he was sitting up again.

"Lay down," she snapped. "You need to heal in the medbed."

"You first," he said, scooting off.

With all the bravado she could muster, she pointed at the bed. "Get back in bed, right now."

He grabbed her hand. "Amaree," he said, pulling her way too close. "You need to lay down before you drop. I'll live. I'm hard to kill."

"I can't do anything until you get in that bed and get healed."

His dark eyes were glossy, though one was still bloody red. His face was messed up, and she knew that he was likely bleeding internally. Not to mention, a third of his lungs were infected. She needed him to get in the medbed. She needed him to heal so she could be done with all of this.

She needed this whole nightmare to be over.

"Please," she begged, not sure why her vision had started to blur. Maybe her eyes were watering. She knew Gammon still smelled, but she couldn't smell anything anymore, either. The vapors had probably affected her eyes.

"Your eyes are closed," she heard him say.

"No, they're not. I can still smell your Grachiness," she said, not sure if she really could. Everything was...fading and she finally realized what was happening. It had been over ten years since she'd had issues with extending her Cerebral abilities. She had practically forgotten what it felt like

The last thing she heard was another whirring sound, then nothing.

SEVEN
DOCTOR DOWN

Gammon held on tightly as Amaree fainted in his arms. He leaned his side against the medbed to keep from falling over. He didn't have the strength that he usually did. He was at least eighty pounds lighter than usual, his body ached, and pain raced through his insides. His lungs felt as if someone had stuffed a rag inside to stop him from breathing. He could feel his adrenaline crashing, not to mention his lack of strength after being chained to a chair and beaten just because the pricks who'd taken him needed someone to hurt.

Gammon hadn't planned on giving up trying to escape, but he didn't really believe that he would get free. The female in his arms had freed him, and that was saying something, considering how untrained she was.

As a commander, he had seen his fair share of battle. He knew the kind of person who could make it and who likely wouldn't. Never had someone so green impressed him so much.

Looking down at the top of her head, he thought about kissing it.

No, to be honest, he thought about rubbing his mouth on it to mark her with his scent.

Gammon held back. She wasn't his bed partner or mate.

When Kava didn't appear after that thought, Gammon wondered if the captain was too busy flying through the asteroid belt to come and interrogate him. Either way, he might have time to get back at the bastard for sending in Amaree to save him. Because, despite being free, Kava still deserved to have his heart ripped out and eaten.

Amaree was starting to slip in his hold, so he carefully rolled them both onto the medbed. He didn't have the strength to lift her. Once their top halves were down, he used his legs to lift hers. It was extraordinarily painful as razor-sharp burns ran up his stomach.

He had been in the Federation long enough to know where the start button for the medbed was. But before he pushed it, he lifted his head at a new scent near the door.

Male.

He turned towards it with a low growl, followed by a fluttering. The medical bay doors opened, and a dark-haired male with an arrogant gaze stood there. Kava. Yellow-eyed bastard. Kava the beheader.

The Cerebral flicked his fingers, and a small, round object came flying from somewhere. It slapped Gammon on the arm and stuck. He recognized the medscope.

"Healing me won't make me want to help you," Gammon said. The pain doubled as his insides slowly healed. Leaving Amaree on the bed, he stumbled out and stood as guard against the pirate bastard.

"Healing you means getting you off my ship faster."

A mix of pain and raw hatred for Kava using an inexperienced doctor made him say, "Didn't know you liked waiting until someone was healthy before beheading them."

"If my mate's job wasn't on the line, I would have let you rot in that cell. You're not that important in my opinion, and I doubt that whatever mission you botched was worth the effort of sending Ree in to get you."

Now that smelled like the truth, and Gammon was baffled for a minute. "Who's your mate?"

"No one you know."

Gammon didn't need additional reasons to hate the bastard, but his arrogance added to his hatred. "Who hired her?" Gammon asked instead, hoping to get something out of the bastard. His mind was clearer now, and he couldn't feel the radiating pain any longer. Standing taller, Gammon realized he was still hungry but not so much that he wouldn't back down to a fight to the death with the little shit.

"Tell me what you are and how you fooled the Federation into thinking you are a Grach, and I'll tell you," Kava said as he moved to the side of the door and leaned up against it, seemingly as relaxed as a male looking for an evening drink.

Gammon saw a series of pans that he could use to bash the captain's head in. It would be the most satisfying fight he'd ever had. Just before he took a step, he smelled something old. Something from a memory. Gammon didn't remember what kind of being the scent belonged to, but he knew it meant death.

A dark shadow rolled up beside Kava.

Gammon's memories cleared, and he knew *exactly* who that was. "Nem," he whispered, knowing his old companion from when they were slaves to a black-hearted Red Demon who traveled all of space looking for fighters that could dominate in the pits.

The shadow receded, and a male formed. The male's face, red eyes, and long hair were like looking into a memory pool.

Nem stood still as if confused. "I smelled you. I smelled your blood. But the last time I saw you, you were dead."

Gammon cleared his throat, looking between Kava and Nem. Kava didn't say anything, and he didn't look smart enough to have designed this meeting. But if Nem were here, what did that mean?

"I didn't die. But it felt like it."

Nem shook his head. "You were dead."

"No friend, I wasn't."

When Nem didn't say anything more, Gammon asked, "Are you his slave?" He pointed at Kava with his chin.

"No. I am free. My family is with me."

That didn't make any sense. "Your family is here? On this ship?"

"Yes. This was my ship. Then he came," Nem said, nodding towards Kava.

That made even less sense. The Maw wasn't known for hosting a Boore family. Gammon would have known because he had interrogated many of its past crewmates. For years, Kava was on Gammon's radar, tasked with finding out who he allied with.

So Nem standing in front of him, talking to him about his family, made Gammon question if he was actually awake.

Taking a hand to his chest, he felt the warm skin and waited to feel the beat of his heart. Looking back at the medbed, he saw the young doctor who'd saved him—in a manner of speaking, at least. She was still there, in the exact spot he'd left her.

This had to be real. It just didn't make sense.

Gammon was not so distracted that he missed a new scent in the air. Female for sure, but not a race he knew well.

"Why are you standing in the doorway?" a female said as she walked around Kava with narrowed eyes. She looked at Gammon and then at Nem, seeming upset. "He's not a threat. You don't have to guard the medical bay."

"Gammon is almost as good a fighter as me," Nem said.

The bastard had only won because he cheated and turned into a shadow. But Gammon didn't say that. Instead, he watched the female he assumed was Kava's mate—they shared scents.

Facing him, she took in a deep breath. "Hi, I'm Fenton."

"I don't know you," he said, making it clear that he didn't trust her.

"I know you don't know me. That's why I introduced myself," she said with a worried expression. "Are you well? Do you need further medical attention? I can see where Amaree is. I'm sure she will..." Fenton peered behind him and then touched a finger to her mouth. Whispering, she asked, "Oh, no. Is she okay?"

Kava didn't whisper when he replied. "Ree is fine, she just had a lot to process."

Fenton shook her head as if she didn't believe that. "Adrenaline crash sounds more like it."

"Same thing," Kava said.

"No, it's not," she said dismissively before stepping in and holding out a hand to the closest Minky screen.

Gammon watched as both Kava and Nem leaned in as if they might follow but didn't. The instinct inside him rumbled as if calling for them to break into his territory. Kava's eyes were on Fenton, laser-focused as if he were fighting himself not to do the Cerebral thing and pull her back.

Gammon figured Kava would prioritize his mate over anything else should something happen. He'd remove her if Gammon moved too fast or even thought something that crossed a line. Nem, on the other hand, stared, ready to attack him if anything went down.

Gammon would attack either or both if they moved to take Amaree from the bed behind him where she slept. His instinct hit him hard, and he knew that Amaree was not going to them. She was his to protect.

"Okay, so..." Fenton said, drawing his attention but not his gaze. "Admiral Rannn says that he is in court and will call as soon as he gets out."

Gammon didn't believe her. It was easy for her to say that she had communicated with the admiral. It was another if he saw the Niking's white face and long, pale hair.

"So, I guess you can take a shower or five and get clean clothes on until then. Do you want me to show you to a room?"

"I'm staying here," Gammon answered, still watching the males at the door.

"Are you still hurt?"

"I'm not hurt, and I'm not leaving the medical bay."

"I'm not sure I understand," she said, walking from the Minky screen to a spot between him and the door. "Why are you staring at them like that... Oh," she said, turning to Kava and then back to him. "Okay, that wasn't expected." Holding up her hand, she asked, "If I go get you an entire cooked dish of food, will you promise to take a shower and put on some clean clothes?"

"Agreed, but the medical doors stay locked while I shower."

Fenton pursed her lips. "Mm-hmm. Okay, but I will stay here to ensure that you don't do anything that might cause my mate to behead you."

Gammon snorted. There was no way Kava would let his mate stay in a locked room with a cannibal.

Fenton cleared her throat and amended, "I revise my deal. Prussia will stay in my stead."

Gammon didn't care who stayed so long as it was a female. His instincts were riding him hard, and he was not in as much control as he would like. Not even close to being on the same level as when he had acted as a commander for the Federation.

His mind understood the rules. His instincts didn't.

"Prussia is a female Ahpaki," Nem said as if answering Gammon's unasked question.

"Then we still have a deal," Gammon announced.

Fenton turned and walked out of the bay, Kava following with a growing scowl on his face. Nem stayed but said nothing.

Gammon wanted to understand how Nem had gotten free of the Red Demon but he figured he didn't want to know more about the Boore if this was all a pirate hoax. Especially if Gammon would eventually have to kill him.

Seconds of silence turned into minutes before Gammon smelled another female. A blue-grey-skinned Ahpaki with thick, black hair cut short on the sides and braided down the middle of the top walked in. Gammon had watched many slaves like her serve the people who'd paid to see him fight.

He looked at the Boore again, not liking the sinking feeling that Nem had lied about everything. About his mate, his family, and being free. Because if Kava had an Ahpaki slave, then he would want Gammon, too.

"I wasn't told what was broken. All Kava said was that I should come to the medical bay," the female said blatantly without being addressed. Ahpaki were known for being proper slaves, even when abused. Why would this one be any different?

"Nothing is broken," Nem answered and then pointed at the medbed. "You are going to make sure the doctor is not touched while the doors are locked."

The female glared at Gammon as if he had already violated Amaree. Walking by him, she spat at his feet and stopped at the medbed, then turned it on so the hatch closed, and it began the healing process.

Next, the impudent slave took a welding gun from her pocket and bonded the two pieces together. Pointing the welding gun at Gammon, she said, "You try and break this bed, I'll break your face."

Then she walked to a door and used the welding gun to point inside. "Come on, I've got a compressor that needs a new filter, and a faulty wire somewhere in this massive ship. The sooner you shower, the sooner I can get back to work."

Gammon wasn't sure if he should be impressed or dismayed. "Kava lets you talk like this?"

Her lips pulled back in a smirk. "He encourages it."

Impossible. Running a hand through his hair, Gammon wondered again why he felt off, like he was actually sleeping. Turning back to Nem, he hoped to get some clarification. Instead, the Boore stepped back so the medical doors could close. Once closed, Gammon walked to the security pad on the wall and manually locked it.

Checking the bay to make sure there were no other ways in, he realized he was finally ready to take a well-needed shower...or two.

EIGHT
ABNORMALITIES

Amaree felt the claws of a deep sleep retracting. A voice that hit like a bolt of lightning struck her mind. "*Get up*," the voice demanded sharply. The blissful sleep called her back, but the voice cut in again. "*Get up, Ree.*"

The bands that kept her in the void snapped away as she floated up until her eyes blinked open. The first thing she saw was blue lights and a canopy.

Was she in a medbed?

More alert, she reached over and pushed the release button so she could sit up. But the hum from the cogs growled as if it was stuck. The medical bed was more plastic with intricate medical wiring that she could mess up if she liquified it.

A female moved to the side of the bed and a hiss echoed in the enclosed space. The canopy was lifted up and set on the floor by a female with bluish-grey skin standing by a door, holding a welding gun across her chest.

The two locked eyes, and Amaree was the first to speak. "Who are you?"

Before the female could respond, she heard her cousin's voice in her head. "*That's Prussia, she's my engineer on the*

Maw. You just got back from rescuing Commander Gammon from the pirate queen. You had an adrenaline crash, and Gammon put you in a medbed. Now that you're caught up, I need you to convince the commander to take a call from Admiral Rannn. Because as of right now, he plans to kidnap you and escape."

Memories of Gammon attacking people in the docking bay flooded Amaree's mind. She didn't get a chance to filter through them before the cleaner door opened, and Gammon walked out wearing black Federation pants, his chest bare, accentuating his emaciated ribs.

At first, she merely observed his form because she was female, after all, but then she noticed that something was wrong with how long his chest was. His ribs...he had way too many.

Amaree tried to remember what his scans had looked like, but the memory didn't come back clearly. Frustrated, she reached up and grabbed the Minky screen, pulling it down to recall the last scan.

Prussia tucked the welding gun in her belt. "Now that you're up, I have work to do." Without another word she left the medical bay.

Amaree could practically feel Gammon coming to stand behind her. His smell was different from when she'd first met him. Instead of the acrid smell of death, she caught hints of spicy ginger, clean woods, and something light and floral. It was surprisingly fresh and sexy as hell.

Taking a moment, Amaree reminded herself that he was a cannibal. He liked to eat people's flesh. He wasn't sexy. Unfortunately, her body didn't care about any of that. It only cared about his delicious fragrance.

She tried to block it out as she looked over his scans, zooming in on two extra sets of ribs at the bottom. Two pairs she hadn't noticed before.

"Why are you looking at my old scans? I'm healed. No need for a checkup."

She stepped in front of him and jerked her shoulder back, hopefully giving him the cue that he needed to back up and let her do her job.

Gammon moved to the other side, brushing her shoulder as he did, making her already sensitive skin tingle at the touch.

Damn it.

"I'm checking again."

"Why?"

"Because I wasn't in the right frame of mind earlier. Now, I am."

He grunted and folded his arms over his chest, not leaving her side.

Leaning away so they no longer touched, she tapped the screen and zoomed in, realizing that his whole bone structure was thicker. It looked more obvious because his organs had shrunk, but that was normal for someone who had been starved.

Crap. He was starved. His organs would need gentle coaxing before he ate whole foods, or he could die.

Looking around, she saw a chiller in the corner. Opening it with her telekinesis, she saw it was stocked full of both water and food packages. She brought them all out and floated them towards the medbed in front of them.

Setting most of them down, she reached over and picked up a water pouch and a packet of tomato soup, handing them to him.

Gammon looked at them and then her. "Do I look like a soup kind of male to you?"

"Are you saying you only eat people?"

He scowled. "Only when I'm starving."

"You bit the people from the asteroid city," she said, remembering the horrid images.

Narrowing his eyes, he said, "When fighting for one's life, you don't fight fair, and you do whatever is necessary to tip the fight in your favor. No one wants to be eaten by another person, so I used that fear to give me an edge. Fighting is just as much mental as it is physical."

Oh.

"So, you *don't* actually eat people for food?"

"No, hun. I don't eat people for food. Not unless I've been starved. And it's been a long time since I've been at that point."

That made her feel a whole lot better. She hadn't let a cannibal loose on the unsuspecting planets and moons. She wouldn't have to live with that guilt and regret for the rest of her life.

"You looked relieved. If I didn't kill you when I first met you, I wouldn't do it now. I'm almost offended," he said pointedly.

She felt bad about that, but he couldn't be that offended, could he? Instead of asking more, she shook the soup packet. "You need to start with liquids, and slowly, before eating whole foods. You can die if you don't. It's one of the things that happens when people are starved."

He took the soup and water and mumbled, "For future reference, I'm not a tomato soup kind of guy. I prefer stews."

Amaree chuckled. Raw flesh had to be worse than tomato soup. "Stews will be too hard on your stomach right now. It needs time to settle."

"You make it sound like the medscope didn't heal me," he said between gulps of soup.

Wait...why wasn't his stomach healed?

Touching the screen again, she zoomed in on his digestive tract. Taking another look, she was sure that his stomach was deformed. It was longer than it should be.

Gammon rumbled a burp. She looked over as he tossed the

two empty packages onto the counter and then grabbed three more bags.

"You don't listen very well, do you?" she said.

He grinned. "I take after you, I guess."

She rolled her eyes and focused on the Minky screen, amazed that the male had made it this far in life. Zooming out, she observed his body again, this time looking for more irregularities. Moving on from the digestive tract, she took a second look at his glands.

She pointed to his mouth on the screen. "Looks like you have an extra set of glands in your mouth. Possibly some congenital disorder," she theorized.

If he were healed with a medbed, it would have set him back to his natural state. And his natural state was this. "Graches usually have gramone glands under their arms and behind the knees."

He slurped on another bag, finishing it off before replying. "If you're trying to impress me with things I already know, it's not working, doc."

Moving the image so the groin was in the center, she pointed to the lack of glands to excrete the addictive hormones that kept all Grach partners addicted. Interestingly, there were none there. With the medbed, they should have been healed. They should be there. "I've never seen a Grach deformity this extensive."

"So I've heard," Gammon said blandly.

She ignored his comment and saw yet another abnormality. "What the hell is that in your larynx?"

"I don't know, you tell me," he said and took another handful of packages from the chiller.

"This isn't right. There are little spores in—" she started, but Gammon reached over and powered off the screen.

In one quick move, she picked him up with her abilities and held him in the air. "What the hell is wrong with you?"

"I've had thousands of scans. I'm done going through this process. Just get it into your head that I'm abnormal and skip to the end. That end for you, however, includes putting me down because I'm not a blowup doll you can carry around."

She didn't want to stop looking at his scans, but what he'd said was probably true. Many doctors would have noticed what she had, and they would have wanted to know more. Lowering him, she remembered that Kava had asked her to get Gammon to talk to Admiral Rannn.

Figuring that she had to escort him to Kava's office, she took a step closer to the door, but stopped short. Gammon's scent filled her nose, which was probably why his skin looked so inviting. Her mind was strong enough to keep her hands to herself, however.

His voice rumbled low when he said, "That's the last time you're gonna do that. Got me?"

She felt the chastisement. More so because, as a doctor, she made it a point to keep her abilities in check and focus more on her knowledge and education when dealing with patients. It was only when she absolutely needed to that she used her telekinesis.

Considering that Gammon was a commander, she should have treated him with more respect. Before she was able to agree, he added, "Next time, I will even the score."

For a moment, she didn't understand what he meant, but then he brushed a thumb over her mouth. Then, she *understood*. He would use his gramones on her.

Forcing herself to remain still, she told him, "I wouldn't try to intimidate me, if I were you."

"If I was *trying* something, you'd know it, hun."

That damn voice mixed with his scent and the fact that her

lips still tingled made her feel all out of sorts. Those gramones really did work.

"I saved you a butter pasta. You might want to grab it for the flight."

Flight?

Ah, yes, he still planned to escape.

"There is one thing you need to do before you leave."

He leaned back, and her eyes were drawn to the movement. His dark eyes, less wild than before, held her captive. Until he said, "I don't think we have time for that," making it obvious that he was talking about a blitz.

In no way was she thinking of that, but now that he'd said it, she *could* imagine them in a cabin, on her bed, under the covers. Her cheeks flushed at the idea of being physical with him. "I'm not going to blitz you. Your gramones smell good, but I'm not a slave to them."

Gammon gave her a knowing look just as Kava's voice entered her thoughts. "*Wrap it up, Ree. I want this guy off my ship.*"

"Let's just go," she said, sidestepping him as she walked to the medical bay doors.

If there was ever a moment in her life where she felt utterly embarrassed, this one topped all of them.

The doors didn't automatically open, and she almost ran straight into them. To her dismay, she watched as Gammon punched something into the sensor with a straight face, but she was sure he was laughing at her.

Her insides started to shake with emotions she had never felt before. With every cell in her body, she attempted to tamp it down. The doors opened, and she walked directly to the elevator. Gammon followed.

They reached out and hit two different destinations. Hers was the captain's office, his was the cargo bay.

"We're leaving, not making rounds to tell everyone goodbye," he said as he hit the stop button and cleared the directions, then hit the cargo bay again.

Kava told her, "*You know...I could have just patched the call into the medical bay.*" No, she hadn't known that, or at least she hadn't thought of it. Frustrated beyond words, Amaree didn't bother responding to Kava. Instead, she kept her face forward as she mentally grabbed the cab and began lifting it up.

The sooner she handed Gammon over to Kava for the call, the sooner she could go home.

"What are you doing?" Gammon asked with a feral rumble in his voice.

She didn't answer.

Moving in front of her, she practically felt his anger. Regardless of how her stomach started twisting with anxiety, she avoided looking at him and continued on with her plan.

"You're not a pirate, Amaree. Stop acting like one. He doesn't deserve your loyalty. Not after where he sent you."

Against her better judgment, she said, "You're right. I'm not a pirate."

Gammon pointed to the elevator controller and leaned in with his voice a rage-saturated whisper, "If you're not a pirate, then take this cab to the cargo bay."

"Since you know I'm not a pirate, maybe you should ask yourself *why* I'm taking you to the captain's level," she said.

"*Do not take him to the captain's level,*" Kava said.

Stopping the cab, she asked Kava, "*Then where do I take him?*"

"Finally, you're getting it. Now drop the cab and let's go to the cargo bay and borrow a ship," Gammon said, dropping his arm and exhaling a breath.

Kava told her, "*I've already ejected the ship you took from the asteroid city. There are no other ships in the cargo bay. But you can take a lifepod. I can patch Rannn through to that.*"

"Fine," she said out loud as she lowered the cab bummed that Kava ejected the ship with her new knife in it.

Gammon moved to the front of the cab as if he expected to be assaulted. When the doors opened, he stepped out and sniffed the air. A second after they were both out of the elevator, Amaree heard him growl.

"That bastard took my ship."

Amaree internally rolled her eyes. It wasn't his ship. It wasn't hers, either. Regardless it would be stupid to fly such a broken vessel. Walking past him, she headed straight to the hall with the lifepods. With a brush of her fingertips, she activated a pod, and the door opened. She pointed at the small space.

He looked at her and peered past her into the cabin. "It's going to be a tight fit. You sure?"

"I won't be going," she said dismissively. "As soon as you get in and go wherever it is you plan to go, I'm going back to my room to shower, pack my things, and go home. I agreed to help free you. I'm done now."

Gammon shook his head and moved forward. She felt his large finger wrap around her wrist as he pulled her in. Stunned at his quickness, she meant to throw him off, but he spun her in the air as if they were falling, then clutched her face and pressed it against his chest, throwing off her equilibrium.

Hissing, she pushed against him.

They landed hard in the pod, with Gammon in the main seat, holding on to her so tightly, she couldn't move or see. She couldn't use her ability because she didn't know the pod's dimensions, and she couldn't concentrate on anything metal to manipulate because her whole top half was pressed against him.

Against her better judgment, she opened her mouth and bit into his flesh.

He growled the same way he always did. Then the bastard put his mouth over her earlobe and bit down. Not hard, but enough to make her fully aware of his addictive gramones entering her system through the skin-to-skin contact.

The bastard.

Pulling away as hard as she could did nothing. And because she couldn't kill him with her telekinesis, because she was a doctor, she only had her average strength.

She formulated the adverse effects. His gramones could be more potent than others because of his birth mutation. She didn't know. The fact that the pirate queen wanted to use it to punish others suggested that it was powerful and that the withdrawal would be spectacular.

The lightness of her stomach said they were no longer on the ship but were instead in space. The bastard had pulled her into the lifepod and deployed it, taking her away from the medscope she needed to cure herself.

Not to mention, lifepods didn't have navigation screens, so she couldn't get back to the ship. Letting go of all her control, she pressed her hands to his chest and pushed back, making sure not to go easy on him. With luck, she could break a few bones.

Frustratingly, nothing broke except a rumble from his chest and Gammon's wild side. His words sounded strangled from a lack of air as he choked out, "Not the 'thank you' I expected."

Hitting his chest again, she would have cursed him but his pecs were rock-hard, and her hand hurt. By Seth's mercy, he let her go, and she stood up in the round pod, holding her hand against her chest. It was the farthest she could get from him, and it wasn't nearly far enough.

Worse was the half-amused, half-concerned look he gave her as he held out his hand as if he wanted to see hers, to heal it or...heaven forbid, kiss it better.

Pissed, she hissed out a breath through her teeth.

Gammon's throat made the whirring noise again, and he beckoned her closer. She was just out of his arm's reach, but if he sat forward he would be able to reach her. The fact that he was calling for her to come to him was...insane. She would never! Never go to him willingly.

But with his stupid bite contaminating her system, she knew the swirling in her stomach fluttering with uneasy excitement of being close to him and urging her to get closer wasn't her but the Grach hormones. Even his smell transfixed, muddying her rational thoughts and filling her nose, warming her insides.

His gramones must be some kind of hallucinogen because she could very clearly see herself crawling onto his lap, knowing that he would hold her—and maybe do other things to make her blood burn.

Ugh.

No!

It was just a reaction to his bite.

"Let me see your hand," he said, speaking with an irritatingly smooth and seductive voice.

"I'm the doctor, remember? I'm fine."

He gave her a condescending nod. "What if it's broken? You'll need me to wrap it or set it for you."

"As if you know anything about mending broken bones."

The side of his mouth moved slightly. "I happen to have years' worth of experience with broken fingers, knuckles, wrists, ribs, and arms pulled out of their sockets. Not to mention cuts, gashes, internal bleeding...the whole gambit of what a body can endure. Now, give me your hand."

She did not give him her hand, but she almost wanted to. She was a doctor who traveled a lot, and she'd come across a few patients known to be scrappers. Each one had a specific set of injuries: fingers, knuckles, wrists, ribs, arms, skull, ears, and jaw. For Gammon to know which ones to name off said he really did know about those things, or maybe he'd suffered those kinds of injuries when he'd been held captive on the asteroid.

Amaree wondered how deep the damage went, then remembered his scans. He didn't have that much remodeling. So he couldn't have sustained those injuries with the pirate queen.

Gammon dropped his outstretched hand and pointed at the bridge of his nose, circling it. "You're making that face again. Where these parts get pinched. Last time was when I let you pull bullets out of my chest. What could possibly be going through your head now?"

She didn't like that he could read her face so easily. But then again, it was good because she needed to know... "When did you get those injuries?"

He widened his legs, getting comfortable. "You're going to have to be more specific. Which injuries?"

Um, did he not remember their conversation? He knew exactly what she was talking about. "The fighting injuries. When did you get them?"

He had to have gotten them before he joined the Federation. The Federation was the only place with medscopes, and if he had those injuries, medscopes would have healed them. Which meant he was probably just a boy.

"Why?"

Why? Why! "Because I want to know."

He smirked this time. "I know you want to know. I want to know why. What will it do for you to know when I was used as a fighter?"

It wouldn't. Not really. But she *needed* to know. "Why does it matter why? What is the point in keeping it a secret?"

He shook his head slowly. "You're cute when you're flustered, but I am still not going to tell you. That was another life. I'm not reliving it."

Another life? For Seth's sake. "Your scans show that you're a little over a hundred and thirty, maybe one hundred and forty years old. Minus the time you've been in the Federation, and the seventy-five years in the academy, you must have been a kid when you were a fighter. As a kid, your brain would have been susceptible to the excess adrenaline and adapted to the abuse..." She covered her mouth, realizing why he fought so savagely. He must have grown up in a savage environment to be okay with turning to cannibalism. It was a defense mechanism.

"Looks like you came up with something," he said smugly.

"I did," she said with compassion.

"Good. Now give me your hand."

Even though he wouldn't be able to fix it, she placed her hand palm-up in his. But because she was a doctor, she couldn't help but add, "It's not broken."

"It's bruised," he said, brushing a thumb over it.

"Not hard to figure that out. It's swelled a bit," she said because she refused to let him think he knew more than she did.

He peered up with another annoying I-know-more-than-you look. "I could smell the bruising seconds after it happened."

Lies.

Pulling her hand out of his, she rolled her eyes. "Graches don't have hyperosmia."

"That's an impressive word. You're definitely a doctor."

With her uninjured hand, she pointed at his face. "Your condescending tone does not disprove my comment. Graches can't perceive odors like bruises. Acting like you do, in front of a doctor, makes you look like a jackass."

He reached up to take her hand, and she snatched it back. "Don't touch me."

Holding up his hands, he seemed about to say something when a ping echoed in the pod. Peering around, she tried looking for the origin of the sound. It pinged again, and she had to fight the urge to check his pants' pockets.

He must have seen where her eyes darted because he said, "It's not me. I don't have a Minky on me."

It pinged again, and she lowered her head, bending over. When it pinged once more, she was sure it was somewhere near her feet. She pointed at his hands. "Keep them up." Then bent her knee and half sat as she scanned the floor. It took another two pings before she found the little cubby under the chair and opened the storage to pull out a Minky pad.

She pulled it up and sat back on his right thigh to read the name of the person calling.

Admiral Rannn.

She internally cursed.

The screen pinged again, and she swallowed, realizing that Kava had purposefully waited until then to patch the call through. He had to have heard their entire conversation. Knew the feelings she was fighting as she sat on Gammon's lap, feeling his warm chest against her back.

He must be so disappointed in her.

"I'm not disappointed in you. And it took this long to get him on the line. The jerk was on the other line with Admiral Orin," Kava said in her mind.

"Admiral Rannn is calling a Minky pad that was stashed in a lifepod for the Maw? That's not suspicious or anything," Gammon said.

She had no idea if Gammon was accusing her or her cousin, but she wasn't listening to it. Straightening her back, she pulled a hand through her hair, making sure she didn't look like someone who was *doing* something in a pod with a very good-smelling male.

"Rannn's mated. I don't think you need to worry about looking good for him," Gammon said with irritation.

She elbowed him in his chest, lightly so she didn't hurt herself. "I was making sure he didn't think I was blitzing you in a pod." Holding up the Minky, she accepted the video so both she and Gammon were in the field of view.

Rannn looked at her and then Gammon and frowned. "Amaree?"

"Admiral."

Rannn looked at Gammon and then her again. "Do your parents know where you are?"

The moments of sheer humiliation kept coming. She wasn't a child. She just turned thirty-one for Seth's Sake. This was why she needed to move out. Even if she rarely went home because she lived mostly on her ship, she needed to be able to say that she didn't live at home. "I don't usually tell them what I'm doing...because I'm an adult."

Rannn gave her such an odd look. "In the words of my old communications officer, 'You're an infant.'"

Up until then, she'd kind of liked Rannn. Now, not so much. Keeping her chin up, she said, "I'm sure Clalls would love to know you quote him. Regardless, I'm sure you called to speak with the commander, so I'll let you two talk."

She moved to hand Gammon the Minky and stand, but a hand wrapped around her waist, and another grabbed the pad. Gammon lowered the Minky to his other knee so Rannn was forced to look up. Amaree wondered if he'd done it on purpose.

"*Yes, he did,*" Kava told her.

"Commander Gammon. I see the mission was successful," Rannn said, sitting back and folding his arms over his chest, looking more relaxed.

Gammon grunted.

Rannn paused as if expecting something more. Knowing Gammon like she did, Rannn wasn't getting more. Apparently, Gammon was stubbornly secretive with everyone. It shouldn't have amused her, but it did. She felt the side of her lip twitch, and Gammon peered over as if he *knew* what she was thinking.

His nostrils flared as if he was smelling something, and she rolled her eyes. There was no way he could smell emotions. That wasn't a thing.

"Your last captain said you were the type of commander to take orders rather than fight them. I see now what that means. So, I'll get straight to the point. Your last mission was botched because someone leaked your location. My weapons and tactical officer was able to find the leaks. This time, I'm determined to use more discrete avenues of communication. Especially for missions like yours."

"Which of your officers?"

"Shady."

"Who leaked my location?"

Rannn paused as he sat forward, taking a more authoritative stance. "Officer Rimmay."

Amaree watched Gammon's face, unable to look away, wondering if it was someone close to him or a stranger. By the slight turn of his head and the clearing of his throat, she assumed that Gammon knew who he was.

In her mind, Kava clarified, "*She. Rimmay and Gammon were bed partners on the ship.*"

Oh.

That was worse. Gammon must have cared for Rimmay. Maybe even loved her.

Looking away to give him privacy for his feelings, she didn't expect him to grab her chin and pull it back to face him. "How do you know Admiral Rannn?"

"My father was on the ship that Rannn, Pax, Yon, and Ansel used to escape Angny."

"What's your father's name?"

"Sci," she answered in the same tone he used with her. "My

uncle Chollar also spent time with Admiral Rannn. I grew up going to yearly barbeques with Rannn and his mate, Yon and his family, Vivra and Pax, Sands, Lita, and their crazy son, plus Ansel, Clalls, and his mate."

"So that's why Kava ended up in the Federation."

Amaree thought of slapping the bastard. How dare he suggest that her cousin hadn't earned his spot in the Federation, *or* that Rannn would allow someone unqualified in the galactic military just because he knew Chollar. Pissed, she said, "I can see why Rimmay would betray you. You're a jerk who probably uses his high rank to disregard facts for your biased assumptions."

His eyes narrowed, and his words were hard as he said, "How in Fenock do you know Rimmay?"

Shaking from his hold, she said, "I don't. How the hell would I know the female you were sleeping with?" Aware of what she said, and assuming that might not be common knowledge to Rannn, she peered down to mute the video call, but the screen was black.

"Look. At. Me," Gammon ground out.

She did, but only to ask, "What happened to Rannn?"

He grabbed her around the waist with both hands, then flipped her to straddle his legs so she faced him. "Don't worry about Rannn. You need to worry about me. How do you know that?"

"I know because you know," she said, being obtuse on purpose.

"Lies. I've tested you from the beginning. You're not a telepath. Not unless you're a phenomenal liar. And no one is that good, especially you."

"I'm a very good liar," she spat, wondering what he had been thinking to try and trick her.

He reached up and grabbed the back of her neck, getting a

hold of her hair too as he pulled her forward. "No, hun, you're not. So, explain how you know about Rimmay."

She did not like the sudden butterflies in her stomach. Being so close with his mouth an easy kissing distance away made her imagine what it would be like. Shaking those thoughts away, she answered, "I told you, I don't know her."

He looked at her mouth in such a way that it felt like both a threat and a promise. That if she didn't talk, he would consume her, pour even more of his essence into her.

Tingles rushed through her body. Heat bloomed in her chest and her lady parts. A growing tide of lust made her want to scoot forward and rub herself against him. She knew deep down that what she felt was fake, but that didn't shake the fact that it seemed very real.

The bastard was playing things to his advantage.

His gramones must make females more susceptible to him. The pull was very real, and the desire to find completion was the motivation. It was a powerful effect, and she wondered how often he used it on other females. She wondered if that was why Rimmay had betrayed him. For making her want him so badly that she just couldn't stand it after he left and was kidnapped. Perhaps she used all her hate to get over the yearning.

"You have three seconds," he whispered and pressed his forehead to hers, opening his mouth.

Her mouth dropped open, and she shuddered. His effect was too strong.

"One, two..." Three had him covering her mouth. His lips were soft, his tongue was not. He dove deep and pulled her close. She tried to move forward but the stupid chair wouldn't allow her knees any farther.

He growled, and she whimpered, needing more. So much more of his body.

Gammon deepened the kiss, consuming her like she knew

he could. No thoughts, just his mouth, his hands, and his taste. She didn't fight him, but she did demand more. And he gave, holy Seth did he give.

She felt something brush her sex. And even though she was dressed, her womb clenched, eager to have him.

"Now," she said without breaking the kiss. She needed him to be inside her. She was hot, achy, and ready. She could practically imagine how amazing it would feel as he drove inside her, stretching her. Good Seth of Stars, she needed this.

She needed more, and the damn pod was in her way. She mentally moved the walls so her knees could push past his waist. Closing the distance, her sensitive lower lips felt his hardness. Curling her hips, she rubbed against his length, and a whole new sound rumbled from him.

"Now, damn it," she said, pushing him down and morphing the metal so it was long and flat like a bed.

Gammon rolled her over so her back was flat. She felt him unfastening her pants. Impatient, she shredded everything separating her skin from his. Gammon mumbled something, but she was far too gone to care.

Legs wide, she waited, feeling him line up with her entrance. He broke the kiss just as he pushed in, and she watched his face as he watched hers. He filled every inch of her as he made his way down her channel. It was at the precipice of almost too full yet not full enough.

Her back bowed when he was all the way inside. She opened her mouth, hoping for more of his kisses, but he didn't lower himself to cover her mouth. He remained above her, watching her with razor-sharp eyes as he began withdrawing. He didn't go far before he backed deep inside.

His hand wove around her neck, pulling her face closer to his. He moved faster in her sleek heat. The carnal scent of their lovemaking hung thickly in the air, adding to the growing ecstasy of being under him, being filled by him, and finding pleasure with him.

Each thrust alternated, short, hard, and deep. It was like he was unwilling to get too far away from her. And she was thankful for that because each time he moved, it brought her closer to her climax.

Getting closer, she pulled her legs back, giving him more space to get deeper. She also levitated just a quarter inch from the metal bed so she no longer felt each thrust inside and on her back.

As soon as she levitated, freeing her from the subtle pain, Gammon pulled out farther, hitting harder, and her climax raced to the cliff. She dug her nails into his arms because they were the only stationary thing she could hold on to.

There. THERE.

Mercy, yes.

YESsssssssss.

She gasped as her climax tossed her off the cliff, and she shattered into a million pieces like a supernova. The pleasure roared through her like a fire, enveloping every inch of her skin and filling her insides.

The hand around her neck squeezed hard, almost painfully. Her eyes flashed open, and she saw the look of sheer, unfettered pain. Gammon's eyes were shut, and she saw a stream of tears flowing down his right cheek.

His teeth ground together, and his back bowed slowly until he sagged to her side. He grabbed his chest as his lips began darkening.

Every shred of pleasure evaporated in that second as she moved from under him and spread the walls out, remodeling the lifepod again. Touching her fingers to his throat, she didn't feel a pulse.

"Oh, Seth," she whispered, terrified that she'd somehow

done this to him. Moving to his side, she interlaced her fingers and began chest compressions. After a count of ten, she checked his pulse.

Nothing.

Cursing, she began more chest compressions, and prayed to Seth of Stars to save him.

After ten seconds, she checked again.

Nothing.

"Don't do this. Please, please, please, please, please," she whispered for all ten of her compressions.

Checking again, she felt a small bump. Relief didn't flood her mind. Something was very wrong with him if a blitz had caused him to have a heart attack. *A heart attack.* Just thinking those words drove a stake of shame into her soul.

She should have seen the signs of someone at risk for heart disease. And yet she couldn't think of a single thing on his scan that had indicated it. Then again, if he were just healed, how did he have a heart attack so soon?

Running a hand through her hair, she grabbed a fistful. What if he was older than she thought? What if he was so old that something this intense could unsettle his heart?

What if she...?

Looking down at him, she realized that he was awake and watching her in silence. Unable to stop herself, she lowered her eyes. "I'm sorry."

"You're...sorry?"

A ball of guilt got stuck in her throat. Swallowing hard, she whispered, "I didn't know you had a bad heart. I didn't mean to..." Flinging her head back because the words felt like thorns, she said, "I didn't mean to cause you to have a heart attack."

In her periphery, she noticed that Gammon leaned on his elbow. "I didn't have a heart attack."

Meeting his eyes, she told him flat out, "You died. Your

heart stopped beating." Jabbing a finger into her chest, she said, "Being with me literally killed you." Amaree could feel the burn in her eyes as tears started to brim.

Refusing to cry, she held them in and turned her face.

Looking at their clothes shredded and thrown all over the many levels of floors and odd crevices that she'd inadvertently made, she wished she could fuse clothes like she could metal.

"I'm sorry," was whispered from beside her.

She shook her head, refusing to hear any more. She knew he was apologizing for using his gramones to lure her into it. But in all honesty, she'd really enjoyed it. It had been amazing until he had the heart attack. She didn't want to hear that he was sorry.

Moving from him, she stood up and felt a cold vibration under her heel. The sensation was different because it wasn't the same material as the pod. She knew what it was before she looked down.

The Minky pad.

She wasn't stupid. The only reason Rannn didn't call back was because Kava must have stopped him. Not being a telepath, the best she could do was call his name in her mind. "*Kava.*"

"*I'm bringing the lifepod back towards the Maw.*"

She and Gammon jerked forward as the pod hit the hull. Lifting her hand, she morphed the pod so it was the right size to travel safely through the hull. To her surprise, Kava had brought her directly to her cabin.

Seeing the familiar room helped.

Without looking at him, Anaree flicked her fingers and pulled Gammon from his spot, then walked through the lifepod directly into her cabin, covering several feet of metal. Once inside, she let go of him and figured she could either hide in the shower or be an adult.

Forcing herself to face him to tell him that regardless of his gramones and the intense pull, she was only sorry for what'd happened to his heart. Nothing else.

As she opened her mouth, Kava told her, "*I probably should have mentioned this before, but he's not a Grach, Ree. I don't know what he is. And he's smart enough to watch his thoughts, stopping me from finding out.*"

A dangerous simmering sense of anger burned inside her gut. Kava should have told her earlier. Much earlier. But even more, Gammon should have told her.

Gammon's nose flared, and this time, she didn't dismiss it. Whatever he was, he could tell what she was feeling. Hopefully, it was telling him to run.

The Minky screen pinged in her room. She peered over and saw that it was Admiral Rannn. Knowing her cousin had done that, most likely to keep her from killing the commander, she figured now was a great time to shower.

And cry.

Or remodel the entirety of the ship.

She got three steps before Gammon grabbed her wrist and spun her around. She had him in the air and frozen a second later. Her words shook with whatever made her insides feel like she might explode. "I suggest you take that call and give me a lot of space. I'm going to take a shower. A long one..." she said and then felt a tickle in her throat. She cleared it and then thought about adding that she planned to pack and leave after the shower, but she couldn't get the words out.

Irritatingly, he didn't sound scared when he said, "You can wait."

"No, I can't," she yelled and flung out her hands. The entire room bowed as she did. Seeing what she had done, she held her breath until her insides started shaking. Her throat tickled again, and she tried to clear it. It took a full cough to get whatever was stuck out.

When she was able to feel secure in herself again, she turned and walked to the shower as delicately as possible, staying a hair above the floor, just in case.

Once the door was shut, she let Gammon down. She stood by the door, waiting for the Minky call to stop pinging and praying that Gammon didn't come to the door. She was not okay, and she desperately needed to be, or bad things would happen.

NINE
A PIRATE'S WORD

Gammon accepted the call and walked out of the camera's view, heading towards a small side table with two piles of clothes in grey and light brown, folded symmetrically. He could tell they hadn't been worn by anyone previously because they had a plastic and oil scent to them.

"Commander Gammon?" Admiral Rannn called.

"I'm here. Getting dressed," he said, unapologetically walking to another shelf and seeing stacks of small, medium, large, and extra-large Federation clothing packages. Gammon pursed his lips, wondering why the Maw would have so many packages...as if Kava had stolen a pallet or two.

Unsealing a large package, Gammon took the white shirt and pulled it on. In the cleaner, he heard Amaree cough again and try to clear her throat.

She deserved to understand what was happening. The problem was, there was a telepath that would undoubtedly delight in informing the Federation what Gammon was to get him kicked out and sent to Debsa.

Gammon made his way to the Minky screen.

"You do realize I'm your commanding officer, right?"

"I know you have a fancy title. But at this moment, it means less than piss. Especially considering you hired the same bastard you fired for beheading an entire ship full of people. I also know he overtook the first ship he happened upon in the Outworlds and continued pillaging and killing on every ship he came across."

Rannn paused for a moment as if deciding how to proceed. Gammon knew enough about the admiral to know that he wasn't overly-sensitive to blunt conversation.

The pale-faced bastard reached up and touched the screen. An image of a person Gammon had never seen before showed up on the far-right side. The person was humanoid, but Gammon had never seen dark purple skin and white eyes before.

"Do you know what race this is?" Admiral Rannn asked.

"No."

"Neither did anyone else up to a year ago, but they are a large one that effectively wormed their way into the Federation ranks and many planets on this side of the wall."

Gammon pursed his lips, not believing that anyone who looked like that could move anywhere in society unnoticed.

"This is a Bezoral."

Stupid name.

"They are named after the one who saved them, Elder Bezoral - The Caretaker."

Gammon didn't know if Rannn had gotten his facts right. "That sounds like a Cerebral name."

Rannn's bushy white eyebrows rose as if to say: "*Does it now? Good for you for putting two and two together.*"

"Why would a Cerebral have anything to do with another race? They lived in isolation until just recently."

Rannn tapped the screen again, and Gammon watched a small clip of Kava slicing his hand through the air, and a series of people and their heads falling to the floor. Seconds later, the admiral stopped the video.

"I don't think there is a person who served on Pegna who *hasn't* seen that video."

"Exactly. The thing is, it's fake. Kava didn't kill that cargo ship's people. There is evidence that proves that not only was Kava not in the area when it happened, but also that the person who witnessed it was, in fact, fed an illusion by a Bezoral."

Gammon dropped his arms. "You're going to have to run that by me again."

"Let me explain it this way. Cerebrals used to continue their population by control, only birthing a set number of babies each year. Every batch, as they called it, was tailored to a specific trade or skill to fill the spot of someone they'd lost."

Gammon didn't know the specifics, but he wasn't impressed. "Very organized of them."

Rannn ignored that and continued. "One year, a scientist experimented, and the result was a batch of babies with white eyes and the inability to communicate telepathically. The council declared them a failure and gave Elder Bezoral the order to terminate them. I don't know if you know this, but being able to communicate telepathically is the one requirement for living functionally in their society."

Gammon held up his hand, making sure he understood what Rannn was claiming. "Wait, are you saying that they killed infants because they weren't telepaths?" As he asked that, he immediately thought of Amaree, who was Kava's cousin. Kava was a Cerebral, making *her* a Cerebral. But when he'd asked her what she was, she'd answered Terran and Kooyon, not Cerebral.

"Yes, that's exactly what I'm saying."

Gammon was still too angry to comment. Those soulless swines deserved to have their eyes stabbed. Being a telepath didn't make anyone more worthy.

Rannn continued. "Instead of killing them, Elder Bezoral took them to a new planet and raised them as his own. As they began to reproduce, they developed a unique trait. The ability to push illusions into someone's mind. Their skill was so effective that he feared for them and told them they would come to kill them if the Cerebrals ever found out about them. And that was the legend that all Bezorals were told in elementary school. And is why they all learned to develop their illusions to keep them safe. To keep everyone outside their planet from seeing the *real* them. They went out and removed certain people and took over their lives. Each Federation person was strategic and the infiltration thought out. Now, tell me, Commander, why do you think a Bezoral would want to have Kava framed for killing a ship full of people?"

Gammon didn't like questions that answered themselves, but the question made sense. "A Cerebral would be able to hear a Bezoral's thoughts. He would know if one was around."

Rannn held up a finger and pointed it at the screen. "Correct. Which brings me back to the video. It's fake. A Bezoral illusion."

Gammon rubbed his face, wondering if he had ever been close to a Bezoral. Smelled one and didn't even know.

"Fenton, Kava's mate, was the one who found the Bezorals' planet and exposed them."

"That's great, but what about the ones hiding like bacteria in the ranks?"

Rannn looked away as if he didn't want to answer, but that was the only option. The only mission that mattered. "First priority would be to find all of them, arrest them, and either send them to Debsa or their home planet." As he said that, Gammon knew that if he didn't keep his mind right, he could be the one exposed.

"It's already done."

Surprised and a little impressed, he said, "That was fast work. How did you do that? Kava?"

"Arvey," Rannn said like the doctor was a troubled kid that was the bane of his existence. Gammon knew that Arvey was a Numan doctor on Pegna, but he didn't talk to him much. When given the opportunity, he usually saw Rannn's mother, who was also a doctor. One that didn't work with too many medscopes and screens. *The old-fashioned way,* she called it.

"What does that mean?" he asked.

"Arvey...designed a virus to destroy the part of their brain that allowed them to push illusions and gave them limited-range telepathy."

That stunned Gammon. "He *gave* them telepathy? As if it's as easy as: 'Here's a pill, thank me in the morning?'"

"More like he detonated an air bomb on a ship and infected everyone who then ended up infecting the planet, who then infected all the planets and ships and space stations. Without their ability, they were all gathered up and taken back to their planet, where they are currently quarantined until the Cerebrals educate them in how to deal with other people's thoughts."

Gammon didn't understand that at all. "The Cerebrals went to teach them to deal with their thoughts?"

"No. Cerebrals are teaching them to deal with *other* people's thoughts. When you're not used to hearing everyone's raw, gut reactions, it creates a deep sense of anger and resentment."

Not that Gammon could understand, considering his hyper...whatever it was called. Peering to the shut door, he kept himself from going over and breaking it down. His damn instincts were driving him mad, worse than before, and the only one who would suffer was Amaree. Especially now.

"Now that storytime is over, let's get back to the mission."

"The mission was a bust the second the details were leaked to the pirate queen" Gammon said with finality.

"Are you saying you're quitting?"

"The Federation? No, not exactly. But the mission is over. The pirate queen knows the Federation is looking to make alliances so we can expand our territory. She knows I was searching for King Azze's son with the intent to get his support for the Federation expansion. I can assure you, she's hunting the son. Most likely she's found him. She'll aim high to get the King indebted to her, and use his support to take over the rest of the Outworlds. You'll have to evacuate everyone from the moons they've laid claim to."

Rannn sat back and rubbed his chin. "That's it? We turn around and go home? Put the wall back up and hope the peaceful races don't all end up slaves to a pirate queen?"

Gammon shrugged. "I leave it up to you. I'm not an admiral."

Rannn reached over and grabbed a Niffy, took a drink, and then set it back down. "All right, well, since I'm *the* admiral and your commanding officer—given your captain is dead—I've decided that you're going to figure out a way to find the king's son before the queen does. And if she's already in negotiations, your job is to break it."

The stubborn old bastard. Gammon shook his head. "There is no way I can do that. I don't have a ship and I lost all my contacts. The queen killed all of them in front of me."

"I understand you're scared—" the admiral started, and Gammon cut him off immediately.

"I'm what?"

Rannn talked over his interruption, "—it's natural after being taken and tortured."

"I am not scared." Gammon cut him off again.

"The crew will assist you," Rannn persisted.

Holding up a hand, Gammon said, "What crew? Because if you're talking about the Maw, you've lost your mind. The Maw stands out like a Bolark in the snow."

At that, Rannn waited until he'd put down his hand, then sat forward. "You have two choices, Commander. Do as I tell you or crawl back into a lifepod and pray to Seth I don't find you."

Gammon stared at the admiral, amazed at how quickly it'd come down to a threat. In his head, he heard the telepath say, *"Tell the asshole to get bent and terminate the call. I know a place you can go where the Federation will never find you."*

Kava.

The bastard would love to see him discharged from the Federation so he didn't have to keep him on board. Gammon was about to tell the admiral that he would take option two, but now...screw the telepath.

"If the Maw is going to help me, then I expect to be in charge of the mission," Gammon said.

"Absolutely," Rannn said with a satisfied smile.

"Not in your life, cannibal. My ship. My rules," stated Kava in his head.

Gammon expected that response. It confirmed the Cerebral would help, instead of hindering the mission. He nodded to the admiral. "I'll call you when it's done."

Without a goodbye, Rannn terminated the call.

Gammon's first impulse was to look over at the cleaner. Amaree was still in there, and she was drowning in her emotions. He needed to call her out and explain, but he couldn't trust Kava not to tell the admiral.

If Gammon somehow found the king's son first and could get back to the Federation with no missteps, he could serve out his last year and prepare to return to the Outworlds with

Amaree to set up a small place where no one—not even the queen's minions—could find him.

The door to the cabin opened, and Kava stood there, looking pissed. The Cerebral flicked his first two fingers, and Gammon was suddenly up in the air, floating like a damn balloon. Why Fenock of Fortune gave them such an ability was beyond comprehension.

Kava floated him down the hall to the elevator. Gammon couldn't move any part of his body, including his mouth. The trip was quick as they made their way to the captain's office, which looked more like a digital game room with so many Minky screens.

Fenton stood in a box surrounded by them.

Once Gammon was on his feet, he thought about punching the yellow-eyed bastard in the jaw.

"I'd crack open your skull before you could move," Kava said, looking at Fenton.

"No beheading?" Gammon said, just to be contrary. When Kava didn't respond, he asked, "Is this the part where you make me a deal to double-cross the Federation and then promise me a planet full of gold?"

Kava glanced over. "You turned down my best deal. You're not going to like my second offer."

Gammon snorted. The Cerebral wasn't a Demon.

"I'm a Silk Demon *and* a Cerebral."

Shaking his head, Gammon couldn't think of a worse combination. A Demon's morals with the power of a Cerebral... No wonder Kava was...Kava.

Fenton was tapping each screen as fast as she could. With one screen, she stopped to scan the contents of something.

"What is she doing?"

"Finding the son. What else would she be doing?"

Just then, Fenton made a sound and slapped the screen.

"Found you, you sneaky little devil." She turned to them and said, "Gabbet. From what I gleaned from the shipping records, journals, contracts, and Federation space scans, I'd say we need to go to Gabbet."

"Where's Gabbet?" Gammon asked. He'd never heard of the place, and he had traveled everywhere throughout his life.

"The Exoworlds," she said with a smile.

The Exoworlds? Was she crazy? "It will take years to get there, and it is not mapped into any system. We could literally run into a black hole, a sun, a planet...the list goes on."

She pulled in her lips as if she were keeping a secret.

"What is that face for?"

She looked at Kava, then back at him. "We kinda have an Exoworlds map."

"How?"

"Antonis," she said as if he should know what or who that was. Then, to his surprise, the door opened. Gammon didn't know if he was more surprised by the unfamiliar scent of a new race, or the male's appearance. He was a few inches taller than Gammon with bat-like wings and a tail with spikes.

Gammon didn't mean to, but a low growl settled in his stomach, followed by a rattle in the back of his throat. The male peered over, exposed his teeth, and made a vibrating hiss that sounded like reeds shaking in the male's throat.

"Stop flirting, you two," Fenton said before pointing to her screen and asking the winged male, "What do you know about Gabbet?"

Antonis looked up and to the right for a drawn-out moment and then said, "Small, blue planet with white trees and purple food. The clouds are always dark, and the people are tunnel-walkers. The bugs eat the tunnel-walkers when they go searching for the purple food."

"Sounds like home," Gammon said sarcastically. But in reality, he remembered his home being dangerous, and food was always hard to come by.

Antonis looked at him and then looked up. "Gabbet is not your home."

Gammon's heart dropped. How did Antonis know that?

"Where is his home?" Fenton asked.

Gammon stilled, waiting for the winged male to answer. He had been kidnapped from his home planet when he was a teenager. His planet didn't have ships or technology, so he didn't know the name or where it was.

Not that he would go back. It was dangerous, and food was scarce. He remembered that much. He couldn't imagine it had gotten any better. *And* it wasn't a safe place for Amaree.

Antonis looked up for ten seconds or so and then said, "His home is not a planet but with his female."

Holy hell. That was true. Did Antonis know what Gammon was?

"Yeah, but where was he born?" Fenton pushed.

"The planet does not exist anymore."

Gammon felt both Kava's and Fenton's attention. He made sure to keep his shoulders back and stood tall to make sure they didn't think he was sad. He wasn't. He was just glad that he hadn't died with the planet. But he did sober to the fact that he was most likely the only Rata alive.

The winged male looked back at Fenton. "Why are you interested in Gabbet?"

"King Azze's son is there. He was kidnapped as a boy, and we plan to rescue him and take him home."

"Do you know his name?"

Fenton touched the screen a few times, pulling something up. Then she looked over at Gammon as if hoping he had the answer. He did. "His name is Oxus."

Antonis looked up and to the right slowly. His wings fluttered and then refolded along his back. A moment later, the male said, "Oxus is not on Gabbet. He's on the planet with the white water and diamond rain. Animal races in the clear tunnels that have paint on their legs. Oxus is a pet to an old Red Demon who grows yellow food in a small shed."

Gammon knew that planet. He whispered the words as his nightmares raged in the pit of his stomach. "Pawwai."

"Yes, that is the name." Antonis nodded.

Fenton touched the screen and smiled. "And it's not in the Exoworlds, that's good. That will make this mission go much faster."

When no one else spoke, Antonis walked out. Kava looked at him and then at Fenton. "Go tell Mung where we're going."

She walked out, brushing her fingers over his arm.

Kava pointed to the Minky desk. "You and Nem have both thought about this Red Demon. Both of you were his slaves. And from what I hear, the bastard deserves to die—slowly and painfully."

"Many have tried," Gammon said.

"I'm a Demon. My word is solid."

"You're a pirate," Gammon mumbled as he rubbed his face. For over eighty years, he had tried to escape the red nightmare, and now he was flying right into the bastard's trap.

"I'm a Demon. I'm a Cerebral. I'm a captain. And yes, I'm a pirate. But you have my word, your old master will die." Kava moved to the side of the Minky desk and pressed the tips of his fingers to it. Up popped a blank note hologram. "I need you to tell me everything about him so I can find him before we reach the planet."

Gammon thought about it. "Nem should be here, too. He spent more time with the master than I did.

"He's already on his way."

TEN

I DON'T UNDERSTAND, BUT I'LL FIGURE IT OUT

Amaree sat in the dry shower, staring at the cold, grey walls, not really thinking, not letting her mind bring back the memories of what it had been like to blitz Gammon. No matter how hard she fought the images, the part of her brain that loved facts thought that now was the perfect time to remind her that Gammon was the best she'd ever had.

It would have been easier to accept that she'd blitzed him because of a gramone pull, but she didn't. She'd blitzed a total stranger who killed without remorse and ate people when starved. That was a hell of a pill to swallow.

The cabin had been quiet for some time. She figured that Gammon was giving her space. A mercy.

Standing up, she planned to accept her actions and move on. Let Gammon know that there would be no more blitzing. No more nothing, because she was leaving. But all that would have to wait because she was feeling sticky in places she didn't want to think about. Tapping *Water*, she selected the preferred temperature and hit *On*. Then she dispensed soap to scrub herself twice.

The cabin was empty.

Folding her arms, she wondered what message Gammon was sending by leaving. Was he actually giving her space? Did he leave because she was only a blitz? Had she upset him by wanting to be alone? Did he think she was irrationally emotional?

Dropping her arms, she tried to keep from feeling too much.

Things like this happened. It wasn't life or death. Whatever reason he had for leaving didn't matter. It was over—even though she'd thought she would be the one to end it.

"Before you leave, I left a gift for you in the medical bay," Kava said telepathically.

As much as she appreciated it, she wasn't in the mood for gifts.

"It's your frostic knife," he added.

Oh. Well, that was different.

She liked her new blade.

Amaree packed up her things, threw the bag over her shoulder, and melted the walls as she walked through them in an effort to keep Gammon from smelling her in the halls—on the off chance the bastard came back to the room looking for her. If he could smell her emotions, he could follow a trace.

Inside the medical bay, she dropped the bag and picked up the frostic knife. She noticed it was cleaner. With a flick of her thumb, she was sure it was sharper, too.

Her cousin was a good person. Holding the frostic knife, she looked around her body, wondering where to put it because keeping it on her body would make her feel better. Especially if she was going back to flying alone.

Remembering a picture from a Sennite model magazine, Amaree grabbed two scalpels from the drawer and molded herself a horseshoe necklace, then she took a pinch from the leg of the nearest chair to make up a clip for the back to counterbalance the knife.

Checking the mirror in the cleaner, it looked good with her black tank top and dark blue pants. She grabbed her travel bag and hesitated.

It felt as if she was leaving halfway through a surgery.

It made no sense, and a part of her tried to reason that she had done what she'd agreed to do. Whatever else happened didn't concern her.

Adjusting her hold on the bag, she looked at the medical doors, knowing she wouldn't use them to avoid Gammon, but an insane part of her was irritated that he'd left her room without a word.

Amaree was sure she was losing her mind. She needed to melt through the floor until she reached the cargo bay. Then, she needed to find a way off the Maw.

That was what she needed to do. And yet, she had a driving need to know where Gammon was.

"He's in my office, working out the particulars of this next mission. As for how to get off the Maw, take lifepod 4-A. Fenton programmed it for the planet Pahorn. There is a sloop there that we parked in case of an emergency. You can take it home."

Amaree's heart warmed. Kava was the best cousin ever.

Tossing the bag over her other shoulder, she didn't get more than a step before she started coughing again from whatever was stuck in her throat. Letting her bag drop, she frustratingly grabbed the scanner, needing to know what the hell it was. Standing still while the scanner hummed and beeped, she tried to think about what she'd inhaled in the lifepod.

In less than a minute, the scan was done, and she was reading the results. It identified swelling in her larynx. Zooming in, she was able to see little slivers.

"What the hell are those?" she asked out loud, then remembered the spores in Gammon's throat.

"Whaaa...that makes no sense. What race would pass spores like that?" Inwardly, she worried they were similar to Silk Demon thorns and that Gammon might somehow be able to hear her words or speak through her.

Since Gammon wasn't a Grach or anything else the Federation knew about, she could only speculate. She didn't know how to get a sample and biopsy it because, again, she wasn't good at DNA coding.

Not to mention, she was the only doctor aboard, and there was no one to help her remove a spore.

Next, Amaree remembered Rimmay, who hadn't died after being with Gammon, so maybe the spores weren't deadly. But then again, Rimmay betrayed Gammon and gave him up to a pirate queen, so perhaps the spores did something bad.

The medscopes were programmed to heal all the Federation races and Cerebrals. No others had been included or updated because Ansel had written the code, and he didn't have access to the DNA to include all the Outworld races.

That being said, whatever happened, Rimmay wouldn't have gotten medical care to fix it or understand it.

The tickle in Amaree's throat was back, and it took almost a minute before she could swallow properly. The rawness and the little rumble in her voice was enough for her to decide that she wasn't going anywhere until the spores were out. She wasn't an idiot. She knew that a medscope wouldn't heal this because the thorns needed to be removed before her throat could heal.

Of course, that meant she had to figure out how to remove the spores without the aid of a local doctor.

Amaree rubbed her face. She figured she had three choices: call Ansel, call Arvey, or make something to fix herself. Being Ansel's protégé, she knew how to write programs and make nanites or organ bots to do specific medical procedures. Those took time, though, and she didn't think she had enough time before Gammon was out of his meeting.

With the hurry, she had to call someone. She reached up to the screen, and her hand froze from a sudden uneasy feeling.

If she called Ansel, he would tell her father, and he would tell her mother. As a mentor, Ansel might also do what he always did and ask her a series of questions to make her figure it out.

She wasn't in the mood for that.

Arvey would know. He had been willing to help her last time, so maybe he'd do it again.

"*You're not calling Arvey,*" Kava said firmly.

"Why?" she asked out loud.

"*Because he's dangerous.*"

"He's a Federation doctor, Kava. He's not dangerous."

"*You're wrong, but you're old enough to know what everyone knows except you. Remember when Arvey used to go to the picnic that we had in the summers with our families, and everyone that your dad used to work with?*"

"Of course."

"*You want to know why Arvey only came once?*"

"Sure."

"*When he found out that you didn't have telepathy, he immediately started thinking about what virus he could make to give it to you. Of course, you were older and had learned to live without it. Sci tried to explain that to him, but Arvey didn't stop thinking about it. Ansel explained it was a Numan thing, and that once Arvey finished thinking, he'd leave it alone. Except he didn't. He waited until he was on the ship home, far enough that both your father and mine couldn't hear. And then he started planning how he'd send you the virus without anyone knowing. I heard him because my range reaches farther. Needless to say, even after your dad and Ansel talked to him, it didn't stop him from trying. You just happened to be with your mom, flying out to Marnak to visit your grandmother. Ansel figured it out and made something that sanitized the air, but the trust was gone. And he ended up using it on a whole race of people just last year, once he tailored it for them."*

Amaree was speechless.

Aside from her whole family keeping this from her, she hadn't known that Arvey was that kind of person.

Apparently, calling anyone was out.

Sliding her hand over the screen, she opened a new desktop and hit the Federation icon. She entered her Federation ID and pulled up her profile, opening the file with all her previous programs and templates. Biting her lip, she quickly scanned through each one, looking for one that was similar enough that she didn't have to rewrite the whole thing.

ELEVEN
LOOK, I'D APOLOGIZE BUT I'M NOT SORRY

Gammon was pretty sure it had been a little over two hours since he'd left Amaree. Considering what she was going through, he needed to get back to her, and he had told Kava all he knew. They were already on their way to Pawwai, and he really didn't want his spare time wasted talking about the master anymore.

That was a different life, and he preferred to focus on this one.

Without a goodbye, he left Kava's Minky table.

"Gammon," Kava called from behind him.

Turning, Gammon said, "It's Commander."

Kava shrugged. "For now."

"You have something to say? Say it."

Kava stared him down as if trying to intimidate him. "I know enough about you to know that I could destroy your reputation and get you discharged right now for lying about what you are."

Gammon knew exactly what the male was doing.

Continuing, Kava said, "If you don't follow my plan, I'll make sure that happens."

"You're not my captain, but I agree with the plan."

"Good. Now just think what I could do to you if you try and pressure my cousin into a life she doesn't want."

Had Kava been any other person, Gammon might have gotten in his face and threatened to eat his eyeballs or something. But Kava was Amaree's cousin, and the fact that he was standing up for his family actually impressed Gammon. "Noted."

Kava immediately went back to speaking with Nem, going over the planet's security and the Red Demon's home, as well as all the secret hallways, training cages, and the underground compound where the Demon spent most of his time.

Gammon left the office and took the elevator down. The second he stepped out, he smelled her. He sniffed the air, seeing how fresh the trace was. It wasn't in the hall, but it was close.

He stopped in the medical bay, smelling her strongly there. Doing a quick pass, he didn't find her. Leaving, he turned to walk down to their room when he realized that her scent wasn't in the hall.

He grunted and walked back into the medical bay, finding her most recent scent. It stopped in front of the Minky screen. Looking down, he knew she was traveling through the ship. The Maw was big, and he had no doubt that he could find her, but what she didn't know was that running from him like this was triggering his animalistic side—his unreasonable side.

Gammon silently stalked through the ship as he made his way to the cargo bay. Instead of running around the vessel like a young pup, Gammon moved to the shadows and waited, knowing that if Amaree was avoiding him on purpose, she was running from him.

No more than twenty minutes passed before he smelled the ozone of the metal wall turning liquid. Amaree walked out from the storage room and into the side hall where the lifepods were. She held a vial of something grey in one hand, her travel bag over her opposite shoulder.

He was right. She was avoiding him...and attempting to leave.

The wildness in him burned inside his chest.

Just as he was about to step out into the light, he saw Amaree casually sniff the air. Then she stopped as if something had hit her chest. She lifted her chin and sniffed again, this time longer. His core retracted in anticipation as her eyes quickly zeroed in on him.

Gammon parted his lips and called to her in his soft trill.

She hissed at him, clearly pissed, but this time he heard a slight fluttering in her throat at the end, like a female of his race did. The sound made his wildness ease. The mating hadn't just taken; it was a true mating. As in, she could bear his cubs.

He could feel his excitement slithering in his veins as he stepped into the light. He growled at her again, watching as she stood her ground and pressed her lips together. She was upset and set on staying that way, but being that she was more precious to him, he would have to handle this with a little more...diplomatic finesse.

Not that he'd ever had it, but he would figure it out.

He was about to open his mouth to address her attempt to leave, when he realized that he was frozen in his spot. He couldn't even speak. Decorum disappeared, and his wildness soared to the top.

He growled harshly, still a sound meant for her but more pissed.

Amaree looked away, and he saw the glistening tears in the

corners of her eyes. Then she blinked them back and walked past, keeping her gaze averted.

He growled again, keeping his alarm from going full-on savage.

"No, you don't get to be pissed," she hissed with the flutter again. "You weren't lied to like I was, and you didn't get infected like I did."

Gammon should have told her about everything, but it'd happened so fast. And to be honest, he didn't think he would end up being mated to her. Yes, he'd planned to keep her as his female because he cared for her, but in his very long life, he had never mated. And given the hundreds of women he'd been with, he'd thought he had displeased Fenock of Fortune and was cursed to live without one.

So, instead of growling, he chuffed as if he were hurt. A sound one of his kind would know, but he wasn't sure if she would.

The telekinetic force drew him back and pressed him against the entrance door of a lifepod. Amaree was at his side but she didn't let him look at her. Her hurt and distrust saturated the air and settled deep in his lungs.

"What are you?" she asked.

His mouth still sealed, he made sounds to let her know that he was unable to talk.

She flicked her fingers, and suddenly his head was free. Peering over at her, he told her, "I'm a Rata."

"I have no idea what that is."

"No one does. We aren't in the archives, and according to the winged male, my planet is gone. I can tell you what I know about my race, but I'm not a doctor."

She hesitated to reply.

He hoped that his confession would ease her.

"What did you do to me?"

So much more than he could have ever dreamed of. But how best to put it so she didn't leave him and fly off in a lifepod, escaping and gaining a big head start on him finding her again—something he would do until his soul left his body? He would never stop looking.

"Why did you infect me with your spores?"

By the gift of Fenock? Honestly, he didn't know why it'd worked on her. "I didn't consciously do that."

"Is that what you tell all your bed partners?"

He made sure to let his sincerity show in his gaze. "You're the only one who has loosened them from me."

"I didn't choose this. Don't you dare blame me." Amaree swallowed and then cleared her throat. "The spores infected my larynx and mutated it. Is this what you did to Rimmay? Is this why she betrayed you?"

Hearing that name on his mate's lips did not sit well with him. "Like I said before, you're the only one who has loosened them, and Rimmay betrayed the Federation, not only me."

"She could have done it to get back at you."

Amaree was young, and he understood that, which was why he worded his next sentence carefully. "Rimmay was a communication's commander, who had many bed partners before me, and at least one after we stopped casually blitzing. Given her rank, she wouldn't have put her career and future at risk because she didn't like how things ended between us."

"And how did they end?"

The irritation in Amaree's voice was a mask for her jealousy. He didn't think he'd ever love that particular scent, but on her, he was more than pleased. More confident than before, he answered, "I returned to my cabin after being given my mission orders to go back into the Outworlds to find King Azze's son and use him to obtain an alliance with the Kinglings, when she showed up. I told her I was busy, getting ready for the next mission."

"That's it?"

"That was the last thing I said to her."

Amaree's brows knit together again as they did whenever she was thinking hard. "When did you tell her about your mission?"

"I didn't."

He watched her again as the thoughts circled.

"Then how did she know?"

How, indeed? "The next morning, I reported to my captain's office to go over my reservations when I smelled both him and Rimmay in his cabin—that shared a door with the office. I assumed she found out from him, but I don't know. Considering that he's dead, I'll never know everything."

"She could have done it because she was bitter at being rejected."

"Rimmay didn't care about me in that way," Gammon said and watched as Amaree's anger flared to life again.

Pulling her travel bag strap farther onto her shoulder, she asked, "How do you know? To sleep with someone, you have to care."

He was not going to instruct her on how untrue that statement was. He had slept with many females he didn't care about. But she didn't need to know that. Furthermore... "Rimmay is a Sennite."

Gammon watched as Amaree lost some of her stiffness.

"Sennites don't mate," he said, just to hammer that notion home.

"I know," she snapped, looking at the door to the lifepod behind him. Seeing her eyes on her escape route pushed him to remember how precarious the situation was.

"There is something else you should know," he said, and her

eyes immediately found him. "You are considerably younger than I am, and I—"

"One hundred and seventy-five is not that old, and I'm not a simpleminded thirty-one-year-old. I accomplished more before I turned eighteen than any other female has on my moon. Your age means nothing to me."

"I'm older than one hundred and seventy-five."

"Medscans can be off by a small degree, depending on your planet's specific solar cycle, but it's not enough to change the fact that even though you are older, it doesn't make me less intelligent."

He liked that she was fighting to stay at his level, but the medscans didn't even pick up that he wasn't a Grach. Why would she trust it regarding his age? For the moment, though, he decided to give her a win. "Fair enough."

She nodded with a hint of victory and then scowled again as if she'd forgotten that she was supposed to be upset. Amaree looked at the vial in her hand and stuffed it into the side pocket of her travel bag before switching it to her other shoulder.

Seeing that, he quickly added, "In all that time, I never once infected anyone, as you say. But more than that, when I tried to mate, it didn't take. Not like with you."

There, he'd said it.

Her eyes widened as she let the bag drop to her feet. "You mated me?"

Smelling the fear tempted him to keep his mouth shut, but he wasn't a bastard, and he wouldn't let her mistake the significance of what'd happened. Looking straight ahead, he said, "I'm an Outworlder. We mate differently."

She was silent for several heartbeats, and he wondered if she understood the significance of that statement.

"The female chooses the male," she said before swallowing nervously.

"The female *accepts* the male," he corrected.

Her chest rose and fell faster. "I didn't mean to."

Gammon took that hit. "The second we left that cell in the asteroid city, I planned to keep you. Only once in my life have I cared and wanted to mate another, but she and I never mated, no matter how many times I tried to make it so." He could smell Amaree's sadness, but he continued. "I believed Fenock of Fortune cursed me for what I had done. I thought I would live a mateless life, which is why I joined the Federation. If Fenock had abandoned me, I figured I could at least pay my respects to the Yunkin god Seth of Stars, hoping for an honorary favor. But in all my years of being in the service, I never even came close to *wanting* someone as much as I wanted you. I decided that I would keep you, regardless if we mated or not."

Pressing her hands together and tapping her lips, the light in her eyes faded for a heartbeat. "Then how did we end up mated when it sounds like you chose me? I honestly thought that it was the gramones making me...the way I was." Her eyes closed as she winced. "I've heard a rumor that Outworlder males feel a lot of pain when they mate. Is that true?"

It felt like someone had reached into his body and ripped his soul in half. "Yes. But that's because Fenock of Fortune opens our hearts to bond your essence with ours.."

Amaree threw her head back and cursed. "Your heart literally stopped beating." She cursed again and covered her mouth. Moments later, she shook her head. Several emotions permeated the air.

"Worth it," he said honestly.

She snorted angrily, and then her eyes glistened, and she turned to blink the tears back.

The moment struck him as one of the reasons he wanted to keep her. Amaree was smart, driven, and skilled, and that didn't account for her Cerebral ability. Gammon knew females like Amaree, ones that relied on themselves and no one else.

Case in point, she was hurting, and she was doing everything she could to take control of her emotions and work through the problem. He didn't want to cut off her control. He wanted to lend her some of his. His kind used sounds to convey how they were feeling and what they were thinking. Taking in a deep breath, he let his chest rumble with a short rising trill and a long finish. The sound of him being proud of her.

"No, don't," she said, pointing at him. "This is so serious. This is..."

He wasn't going to let her think that this was a bad thing. Especially since, to him, it was a miracle. Opening his mouth wider, he trilled at her again. More frustrated, she squeezed her fingers into fists and pressed them against her chest as if she were trying to keep from reacting like last time—stretching the walls.

"Let me go," he said evenly.

Amaree wouldn't look at him when she shook her head.

"Amaree," he said, gaining her attention. He wanted to demand that she let him go, but he took a chance and told her, "That sound you make, from the spores? It gives you the ability to call me. It will affect me the same way my call does you."

"I don't make that noise," she whispered as if saying it louder would make it untrue.

Confidently, he instructed, "Think of me. Not my name, not my rank, just focus on me. How I make you feel." He gave her a few seconds to process that before saying, "Now, open your airway and call to my soul."

She shook her head.

"Try."

"I wrote a program that will remove the spores, and my medscope will heal the mutation. I can reverse this."

That was not what he'd expected her to say, and the hit gutted him.

The reality of what she'd said turned his miracle into a hell he didn't know existed—and he'd lived through hell before. As a slave, he had been treated like a pet that had to beg to get scraps of rotten flesh to eat or starve. In the fights he had been thrown into, he had to win because they were battles to the death. If he died, he risked being fed to the other master's pets.

He wasn't even seen as a person then, yet he'd felt more alive than he did hearing his mate...his *true mate* telling him that she was going to break the mating.

Gammon was so stunned, he didn't move, even when she freed him from her telekinesis. A lump grew in his airway, and he had a hard time breathing. He cleared his throat, pushing down the lump, and told her, "Right. Well, that's your choice."

Shutting everything down, he gave her his back. She might have his soul, but he still had his flesh, and he planned to finish the mission. After that, he would keep breathing and keep living and figure it all out one day at a time.

A feminine growl carried in the air and pulled him to a stop. He didn't dare turn around. She'd made her choice. He didn't want to hear her apology or explanation. He understood.

Another growl, this one crushing because it was his. He knew it...felt it.

Fenock had to stop this torture. Gammon could take the beatings, the starvation, and the sickness, but this hollow death consumed every part of him. A blackness had reached inside to squeeze the air from his lungs.

"I can't breathe," she said, followed by a thud.

Gammon whipped around in time to see her head smacking the cold, hard grates. Lunging, he rushed over, his lungs closing up. His mind fogged as he grabbed her head and pulled it into his chest, feeling something slicing into his hand. Bleeding, he found her frostic knife and ripped it off the necklace it was attached to, throwing it towards her bag. Her body was limp, and he nuzzled her cheek, unable to think of what to do. Ten terrifying seconds passed before she gasped loudly.

Pressing his bleeding palm to his thigh, he felt his chest finally ease, and he too took in a long breath. Tingles raced through his blood, filling his cells with oxygen. Amaree's little nails clutched at his arm. He pulled her farther into him, against his chest. She lowered her head, curling tighter in his hold.

"I'm sorry," she said breathlessly.

He had no idea what she was sorry for, and he really didn't want to know.

"I made the nanites so quickly, had them ready, and I couldn't take them. I couldn't lift the vial to my mouth. Every time I told myself to leave, I felt like I couldn't because I was forgetting something," she said, and he didn't know how to process what she was confessing. "You infected me. You mated me, and I had no idea. I'm so mad. I'm supposed to be livid, but I...I was madder when you left without telling me. I was upset that you didn't find me like you should have—like I wanted you to."

The lump was back in his throat.

"I don't like feeling this much," she whined.

Hearing that, he chuckled. "Same, hun. Same."

She lifted her head some, but not to where he could see her. Just feel her. "I thought I was dying. I've never heard of that happening to...people. To people like us."

Mates.

She couldn't say the word. It was another sign to Gammon that she wasn't ready for any of this, yet he was beyond ready. Fenock was a black-souled harpy for bringing Amaree into his life.

"Outworlders are different," he said, not sure if that was the reason or not. All he knew was that he felt the exact same, and he had no idea why.

She got quiet, and he stayed silent, just taking in her scent and soaking in her warmth. He didn't care how long they sat there. He didn't care that his legs were numb. He planned to stay there until she was ready to get up.

"Did I ruin this?"

The hollow voice practically cut him in two.

"No," he said, not sure if she was sticking with her plan to break the mating, or if she had accepted him. Again, he wasn't sure he wanted to know.

"I don't..." she whined. "I don't know how to do this... be your...mate. I haven't ever really even dated anyone, so I don't know what the rules are. And I can't be with someone who eats people."

"There are no rules, outside of you accepting me. If you don't want that, then it doesn't matter what the rules are or what I did to *survive*. You already know how to break the mating. Once you do that, we will figure out the rest."

She got quiet again, her head dropping down to her knees.

"I'm more than happy to hold you, but you need to think about what you want," he said, breaking the silence.

"I'm not overly emotional. I've worked in so many emergency situations, seen so much senseless death and pain... I don't understand why this—us—makes me this way. I swear I'm not like this. I'm very level-headed, even under serious stress."

He kept his amusement from his voice as he put pressure on the top of her head, pulling her closer. "Are you worried that I fell for your emotionally irrational side?"

"Yesssss." She pulled away, looking him straight in the face. Her eyes were rimmed with red, but he didn't smell tears. She had held them in, and he kind of wished she hadn't. He would have wiped them away and made a vow to himself never to make her cry again.

Grabbing the back of her neck, he saw the passion burst to life in her eyes as he pulled her close, but not enough to feel the pressure of her soft lips or to taste them. "I wanted you because you were smart, skilled, and motivated. I wanted to protect you despite the fact that you have abilities that can protect you just as well as I can. I wanted you because my soul called out to yours, and you heard. You responded to my mating call. You responded with all of your body when I kissed you. I was all in."

He felt her hand press against his chest. Worry puckered her brows. "Was?"

He didn't clarify. She was smart. She would get there.

"Can you be again?" she asked.

"Not if I'm in it by myself."

"You won't be. I'll be with you."

Teasing her, he asked, "You *will* be?"

"I'm in," she said, pulling his shirt as if that would bring him closer.

He nipped her lower lip, falling insanely for her as he confessed, "Me too." Covering her mouth, she was quick to move them into the lifepod and straddle his lap. He didn't fight when they were in the air again until she broke the kiss and looked around.

"What?" he asked.

Then he heard Kava's voice. "*You are not ruining another lifepod. You have a cabin for a reason.*"

Gammon saw Amaree's cheeks instantly turn red. Covering her mouth with one hand, she flicked her fingers with the other, and they instantly shot up to the ceiling and melted through the levels until they were back in their cabin.

"Mattress on the floor, hun," he instructed. She smiled, reached out, and mentally pulled the mattress from the bed.

Then she looked him over, and her expression fell. "What happened to your hand?"

"Not a thing," he said, pulling her down and rolling on top of her. Her thighs widened, and he fit right where he wanted to be. Deepening the kiss, he growled. Feeling ravenous for her mouth, her body, and needing to saturate every inch of her with his scent.

Breaking the kiss, she said, "I need to look at it."

"No, you don't," he said, kissing down her neck and nipping at the skin, earning a rumbly female growl. It wasn't her call to his soul, but a growl encouraging him to keep going. Just hearing her sounds did something to him. His sex was already full, hard, and aching, but hearing her growls made him feel as if his dick was getting bigger. Heavier.

"Please, real quick," she said.

"You first, then me," he replied, leaning up to remove the layers between them. He got as far as touching the hem of her shirt before it fell apart, along with her pants and all of his clothing.

"Right. Remind me to keep a storage of extra clothes."

Amaree grabbed his neck and pushed him down with her Cerebral strength. His back hit the mattress, and just before she threw a leg over his waist, he rolled back, flipped her to the side, used his knee to spread her legs, and then repositioned himself so she was mostly on her stomach but with one leg bent so he had deep access and a great view.

Another growl rumbled from her throat, a demand for more, and damn if his body didn't supply it. He knew he wasn't crazy this time. He felt even heavier, and when he hit deeper, he knew something felt different. But every part of him buzzed like little pinpricks of electricity.

It took him a few times to adjust to the right angle to hit her spot just right. His instincts rejoiced as hisses replaced her growls, turning to curses, which turned to moans.

His mate was vocal, and he loved it.

Lying on his side and taking it a little slower, he rubbed her side and then slid his hand between her thighs. He circled her lower petals and found the pearl, then slowly coaxed her as his dick plummeted.

Her little nails curled into his skin. She held her breath. He nipped her ear and rumbled deep in his chest so she could feel it—and respond to it. Just as he suspected, she gasped, and her tight sheath clutched him like a vise.

Damn, the growl worked better than anticipated.

"How do you do that to me?" she asked, turning around and moving on top.

Finding his home, he entered without delay. He tried to thrust again, but he was frozen. His mate, taking full control, peppered his jaw with kisses and nips. He didn't want to slow, and as much as he loved how she rubbed her mouth all over him...

She was marking him.

That was unexpected.

He forced his body to relax and let her do what a mate needed to do. All he truly had to do was stay hard for her.

"You smell so good," she moaned as she moved her hips up and down, concentrating on his tip. If he didn't stop her, he would go in seconds.

"Wait," he hissed, and she hissed back as she dug her nails into his skin again. His whole body jerked as pleasure ripped through him, taking his breath and filling his mate with wave after wave.

She slowed, and he ran through a list of things to do to get her to come, but then she began moving on him again. His sex was sensitive as hell, and it almost hurt. He opened his mouth to tell her to wait, but then she closed her eyes and growled, and his fucking body *responded.*

In an instant, he was hard, and his need to fill her was there again.

That had never happened before.

Leaning over, she kissed him, and he felt the second her hold on him lifted. Rolling her over, he didn't give her a second to adjust. He pulled out and rocked back in as hard as he could. Not because he needed to go but because he needed her to.

She grabbed his neck. "Yes, yessss, that way."

She liked it like a savage...so he gave it like one, taking no prisoners, giving no mercy. He hit as hard as he could, as often as he could, for as long as he could.

Her noises filled his ears, and he kept going.

Her channel fluttered—she was getting close.

"Gammon," she moaned, but he was too far gone to find out if she was just calling his name or if she needed something. Good Fenock, he was there again. She needed to be there.

Please, let her be there.

Amaree cursed right before she bit into his shoulder. His home inside her pulled him deep, and he flooded her for the second time. His vision turned black, but his body was full of white stars of ecstasy.

With her arms and legs wrapped around him, he didn't move. He simply rested his head and let the last of his seed enter her. Closing his eyes, he planned just to absorb the moment. Her fingertips lightly brushed over his back, lulling him into a peaceful, healing sleep.

TWELVE
JUST THE THREE OF US

Gammon didn't plan on waking up in the same position, in a darkened room with the sound of his mate's little snores.

When had he ever fallen asleep like that?

Withdrawing from Amaree's arms, he noticed he was no longer inside her, but that his dick had returned to its original resting size. Creeping from the mattress, he checked the cabin for any scents that weren't theirs. Restless, he wondered what was making him feel uneasy.

Kava's voice entered his mind. "*We're closing in on Pawwai. You have five minutes before we enter the atmosphere.*"

Gammon's unease turned to alert as he turned and headed to the cleaners. One thing he wouldn't do was let the master's pets smell his mate. He had done that before—one of the many things he shouldn't have done—but he was starving and wanted food, so he did what he could to make the master happy.

The master.

Gammon hoped he was the one who took him down, because he would revel in ripping the red bastard open and eating his heart. His liver too. The plan didn't detail such a thing but plans had a way of getting sidetracked or evolving.

Fenock had to be on his side for this mass-killing. Hopefully, Fenock hated the Red Demon as much as Gammon did and would set things up so Gammon could be the one to taste his tainted, black-hearted blood.

Seeing his hand, he realized that not only did the scab look good, he didn't remember seeing blood all over his hand and legs from when he'd bled all over himself and Amaree as he refused to stop the growing intimacy.

Did she clean him up?

How had he not noticed?

In the cleaner, he turned off the water, still looking at his hand, not remembering and wishing he hadn't scrubbed off his mate's scent. He would have been able to tell how recently she had tended to him. *If* she did tend to him.

His skin was wet and raw when he stepped out into the cabin, wearing a towel. Amaree sat cross-legged on a chair with a bag of hot tea on the table next to her as she skimmed past a page on her Minky pad. The mattress was as they had left it, and their clothes were still in shreds. However, the sheet was clean and a completely different color than the one they'd used before he passed out.

Clearly, the wrinkles answered his question. She *had* tended to him, and she did clean him up while he slept.

He had *never* slept heavily. Never. Confused by the mounting evidence, he cleared his throat and said, "You're awake early."

She sat up and shrugged.

"Did you sleep okay?" he asked, wondering why he felt like something was off, but nothing about her scent said so. Grabbing a fresh packet of clothes, he pulled them a little distance from her just to ensure that she didn't notice that he'd scrubbed off her scent. If it were the other way around, he would be pissed.

When he finished, he realized he hadn't been in a relationship in hundreds of years and didn't know what to do or say. Defaulting to his commander's protocol, he told her, "The ship landed on Pawwai. Kava, Nem, and I will do what we have to and get back as soon as possible. Antonis should be staying here, so he will be able to keep watch over the ship until we get back. I don't know how bad it will be, so it is a good idea to stay in the medical bay for when we return."

"I figured," she said, reaching for the hot tea. Before taking a sip, she sniffed the air, and he smelled her confusion. She didn't say anything, and he hated the unsaid words.

He was about to explain that he hadn't washed off her scent because he was rejecting her, but Kava's voice spoke forcefully in his head. "*She's not mad at you. She's just not a morning person. She's up because she wanted to see you off and be supportive. Let's go, for the love of Seth. The two of you are driving me insane.*"

She wasn't a morning person?

He liked knowing that. He also liked the idea that she'd gotten up just to see him off. Needing to reward her, he took a step forward, wanting to kiss her. But then he remembered that he didn't want her scent to be on him.

Damn.

Amaree stood and quickly went to the packages of food, holding one up. "Do you want me to heat something up? Or do you prefer to do whatever you're going to do on an empty stomach?"

"It doesn't need to be warm. I can take it with me," he said, knowing that she would probably hate the idea that he planned to eat the master's liver—or at least rip it out of the Demon's body. He wouldn't stop until the male was unrevivable.

"Oh, okay. Uh, what do you like for breakfast? I don't eat before a big surgery."

He loved knowing that she got nervous before a big surgery. In most of his missions with the Federation, he didn't feel peace like he did now. "I'll eat whatever you grab."

"Okay," she said, quickly grabbing two bags from the chiller, then putting one back and switching it for another one.

When he read the label, he asked, "Which one did you put back?"

"Apple pie. It's too early for something sweet."

It was never too early for that. "Thank you," he said, wanting to kiss her, hold her, and have her scent on him. But he couldn't. It wasn't smart.

Amaree bit her lip, and her brows pulled together. He didn't know what she was thinking but he had to tell her... "Where I'm going, the people I will be fighting, could smell you on me. If they get away, they could hunt you by your scent."

A small smile pulled at the corners of her lips.

"Be safe," he said, meaning it with every part of his soul.

"You, too," she said, waving her hand.

Leaving the cabin, he chugged down a cold stew package. He didn't expect the heavy scent of her cousin in the halls. Kava waited at the elevator with pursed lips. "You want to know what's worse than hearing a six hundred and forty-three-year-old male getting with my cousin?"

"Don't care," Gammon said as he broke the seal to the water package.

Kava waited until Gammon had joined him in the elevator to say, "The answer is, hearing a six-hundred-and-some-year-old male talk about eating someone's heart and liver and knowing that same person kisses my cousin." The doors shut, but apparently, Kava wasn't done. "Thankfully, you're planning on hiding that side, and Ree won't tell her parents because she's not stupid. If she did, they would blame all of this on me. So, this eating organs thing you're planning will be our little secret. The two of us."

"Fenton doesn't know?" he asked curiously.

Begrudgingly, Kava said, "The three of us, then."

The elevator doors opened to the cargo bay, and Gammon saw Nem. Gammon smiled. "Nem knows I've eaten people before. And that it's acceptable to eat the organs of those you hate more than any other being in all the 'verses."

Kava glared at him. "The four of us are the only ones who know."

"My mate knows Gammon is a cannibal," Nem said as he turned to the ramp where they would disembark the ship.

"I hate you both," Kava said as he walked in front of them. Then he finished, mumbling, "Considering I'm about to help you fulfill your fantasies of killing the master, I'd expect you to be more serious."

Gammon looked at his brother-in-arms and grinned.

Nem smirked.

Gammon watched as Kava took one step out onto the ramp. The air barely moved, making the smell of rotting bodies mixed with space dust overbearing. Black marks and old blood still marred the landing pad. Surrounding the quarter-mile slab were thick trees and white flower bushes, giving the impression that it was a welcoming place—a façade.

The sun was high in the sky, and the heat told Gammon it was in the dry months.

Blood rushed through his veins. His fingers stretched and contracted with anticipation. Nem had to be feeling the same rush of adrenaline, because the male turned to a black shadow and growled.

Kava scanned the surrounding area.

"If you needed to mentally prepare for this, you had hours, Cerebral," Gammon said, sniffing the air.

"I can count on my hand how many people I can hear telepathically," Kava said, spreading his fingers out again.

Gammon didn't get the point of that comment.

"My Cerebral reach is like the sun. Everything the light touches on this disgusting planet. That's how far I can hear and see. The fact that only four people are within my reach, and all of them are escaped slaves hiding in caves and remote areas, means I think it's safe to say this will be fun for all of us."

Kava was talking about an ambush, but Gammon couldn't get over the words: everything the light touches.

Gammon couldn't process that, but he would absorb that later when he wasn't getting an uneasy feeling that something was wrong. The summer festival should have brought racing hoppers and smoke from wheeled vendors.

The city was just over the first set of dunes. It was an easy five-minute run. The master had to know they were coming.

Thousands of people came to Pawwai to enter the races and fights. If they weren't here, there was a reason.

"Who wants to play bait?" Gammon said, realizing the trap.

Observing Kava, who turned back towards the cargo bay, he added, "What?"

"Change of plans," Kava said as the freed Ahpaki stepped onto the ramp.

Gammon didn't like where this was going. "No. It's dangerous. Nem and I know where we're going and can get there and back quickly."

Kava didn't seem to hear him. "Prussia is going. She has experience being a slave. She will be able to talk to Oxus in a language he understands."

"I was a slave. Nem was a slave. We understand the talk." Drawing a line, he added, "She's not coming. She'll slow us down."

"My ship, my rules. My plan."

Bloody bastard. "You don't change plans at the last minute, Kava. Even you should know that. It's bad luck."

Kava eyed him arrogantly. "The saying goes, you don't change fighters last minute. This isn't a fight."

"Fine," Gammon said, figuring that Prussia could follow him, and Nem could bring up the rear. Jumping down the side ramp, he let out a growl. Just as he was about to touch down, he noticed the fake black marks on the uneven ground.

He stopped falling, hung in the air for half a second before floating back up. He wasn't replaced on the ramp, and Gammon thought this was Kava getting back at him.

Kava flicked his fingers, and all the trees surrounding the pad tore from the ground and moved to the landing pads. As each tree set off the traps on the pad, a series of six-foot-round metal hunting traps snapped in the air like starving fish with teeth.

A strange electronic wobble hummed. Gammon stared as the first set of dunes receded to reveal a white ring that surrounded the entire dock.

Holy Fenock.

Gammon dropped from the air as a bottle-sized torpedo zoomed from the device. Kava snorted as he slapped his hands in the air, and the weapons exploded.

The device hummed louder and spat out a new horde of projectiles. Kava floated above the ship, and Gammon watched as the torpedoes came from all directions. Gammon's heart stopped as he thought about Amaree still inside. Someone had to stop that massive artillery of death before everyone inside died. Kava couldn't keep it up forever.

Kava's voice said in Gammon's head, "*I could do this for months, it's not even a chore, but this might be a good thing.*"

Oh, was it?

"*I have another idea.*"

Holy Fenock, the Cerebral was testing his patience.

"You and Nem focus on getting the master, and Fenton will take Prussia to get the son."

"You're going to get your mate killed," Gammon yelled.

Kava didn't look at him because of the many incoming torpedoes, but Gammon did see the annoyed expression on the Cerebral's face before the words, *"Just do as I say,"* echoed in Gammon's head.

Gammon peered over at Nem, who watched the torpedoes. "Nem," Gammon called before continuing towards the device. Five feet from it, his stomach dropped suddenly as Kava picked him up telekinetically and tossed him over the machine. Scanning the dunes, he noticed the empty arena and the bare bones of where the festivals were usually held.

Taking the back path, he slowed just as the ground split open and out rushed a blue scathy barbist—a massive snake with a head the size of Gammon's body. A graze from the venomous fangs would kill him in a manner of hours, liquefying him from the inside out.

Falling back, he rolled to his left. To his right, he heard Nem's Boore scream. Keeping the momentum, he pushed to his feet and grabbed a handful of sand as he lunged after the beast currently snapping at the shadow.

Gammon chucked the sand at the thing's eyes. Its mouth opened, coming down on him. Waiting until the last moment, he fainted to the right and punched the thing in the side of the head. Nem jumped onto its back and slashed open the scales.

The barbist knocked Gammon over as it reacted to the severe wound. Once again, the beast snapped at Nem, giving a perfect opening for Gammon to leap up to its lowered head. Digging his fingers into one eye socket, Gammon tried to dislodge the eyeball as he took a bite out of the wet, squishy organ.

The beast screamed again. Gammon was about to take another bite when the head flopped at his feet. Standing straight, he looked at Nem's shadow, still chewing as he said, "That was faster than last time."

The shadow solidified, and Nem's upper lip curled. "I never did like the eyes. I prefer the intestines."

"Those are good, too," Gammon said, hoping his mate wouldn't consider him eating a reptile the same thing as eating a person.

Nem turned back into a shadow as another section of the earth opened, and five shirtless Night Demons with the master's paint on their chest jumped out. As they ran towards the Boore, Nem flashed solid and told Gammon, "Go on, I'll catch up."

Gammon took off, moving away from the stone path that led to the master's front door and looking for the hidden door that led to his underground home. It was only by the grace of Fenock of Fortune that he had escaped the underground compound by finding the stairs that led to the secret door.

Running past, he saw the large, wooden poles with several faces carved into them—each one in a state of agony. Past the poles was the lake of bones. Clay squares had once flattened it, but in the hundreds of years Gammon had spent as a pet, he'd witnessed the smattering of bones extend farther and farther until the whole dry lake was covered.

Unsurprisingly, there were more bones now than when he'd escaped.

Taking a roundabout way to avoid any more traps, he found the area where the secret door should be. Instead of a flat layer of dirt, there was an actual black lake with slow-moving bubbles. It smelled like coal and liquified moss. It was hard to pinpoint the scent, considering he didn't know what it was exactly, but it could be tar. In the center of the lake was a series of spikes in a circle with four bodies impaled and rotting on them. The door was in the center of the spears, but instead of wood, this one was metal.

As soon as Gammon turned to see how far away Nem was, he heard the cogs begin to move. Turning back to the door, he watched as the circle with the master's symbol twisted away to reveal an opening. Black shadows emerged, one by one, first circling the small platform until four stood under the rotting bodies.

They all screamed in unison, a high-pitched screech that curdled Gammon's blood and hurt his eardrums.

Cursing, he bent a knee and grabbed two bones—one for each hand.

He could have taken out one Boore.

Two...would have come down to luck.

Four was a slaughter.

He wasn't in an arena, and he wasn't fighting for pride. This was a job, and he wouldn't sacrifice himself for honor or anything stupid like that.

Just as he was about to call out Kava's name to let him know to send reinforcements, he smelled Nem. His situation became infinitely better.

A second later, bones crunched as Nem stood beside him. "The master redecorated while we were gone."

Nem snorted as he sniffed at the four shadows. "They can't cross this black lake, and neither can I."

"I thought you could go anywhere in your shadow form."

"As a shadow, my body is separate, but it can still feel pain, and it can still burn."

"Great, then how do we get across?" Gammon asked. "That's the only way in."

One of the four shadows solidified. He wore a collar, like all slaves, and he looked half-aware and half-starved. His pants were the only article of clothing that covered him. Gammon remembered those days. The male bent down, flipped open a flap, and then pressed something. Seconds later, Gammon heard and felt a small vibration.

Standing straight, the unnamed Boore curled his upper lip. "Too bad you didn't bring more with you. Even the both of you won't feed us for long."

Gammon was not surprised the Boore spoke. The Red Demon made sure all his pets could communicate, meaning all the Boore got a voice box.

The black tar began moving and a platform rose from beneath. The Boore who'd spoken faded back to a shadow and then screamed. The other three followed suit with the ear-piercing sound.

Stepping back so he wasn't an easy target, Gammon found his spot as the four guard pets ran straight at him and Nem. His body tingled, and his vision tunneled. Just like in every fight he'd ever been in, there was no option to lose. He had a mate and a life, and he wouldn't give them up.

The first Boore went straight at Nem. The second came at him. Gammon's body moved quickly, slashing at the shadows, hoping to hit something important. Another shadow jumped past his periphery, and Gammon gave it his back. Sadly, the bastard slashed open his skin with his claws.

"Mmmm. You taste good," said the Boore from behind Gammon.

Ignoring the fact that the Boore had shredded his skin and was eating it, Gammon figured the Boore was solid, so he threw a kick back, and the male fell on the bones, turning to shadow instantly.

Someone knocked Gammon forward. His hands and knees hit the bones as a shadow engulfed him, taking a bite out of his shoulder. Bellowing, Gammon tried to roll away, but the shadow wrapped its body around his.

A tightness around his neck cut off his air, and another shadow at his feet held him tightly while ripping off his boots.

"Toes are crunchy and juicy."

Gammon roared as he tried to kick his attackers to loosen himself, to avoid being eaten alive. He swore to Fenock that he would never eat another person if he lived through this.

"Gammon," Kava shouted in Gammon's head.

Gammon roared as he grabbed the first bone he could reach and stabbed the Boore in the neck, just as the beast turned solid and took a bite out of Gammon's shoulder. The Boore's blood sprayed over Gammon's face as the second Boore screamed. The other one was still in shadow, looming over Gammon as it ripped off its dead comrade.

Gammon prepared for the attack, but the shadow didn't move. A slight hum rent the air as thousands of bones shot from the ground and into the shadow. There was a scream, and the Boore solidified with eyes wide and blood flowing from all the wounds.

Letting his head fall back against the bones and taking his first relieved breath, Gammon asked, "Now you help?"

"Shut up, I'm sending help," Kava said.

Gammon peered over to see Nem looking over his hand that had three missing fingers. His fighting brother looked just as tore up as he felt, but he was alive, and that was all that mattered. Everything else would heal.

Nem's red eyes found Gammon's, and with a quick nod, Gammon sat up, feeling the fire in his veins. With effort, he pushed himself up while asking, "Who?"

Kava didn't answer. Gammon hoped to Fenock that the Cerebral wasn't stupid enough to send his mate to him. Putting her this close to the master would mean real danger. Then he smelled the Exoworlder before he saw the black-winged being flying at him.

The winged male didn't stop. Instead, he dropped low enough to grab them and fly them over the black tar. It wasn't until they were to the round surface that Gammon realized the raised path the other four used was gone.

Antonis held out his hand. A medscope lay on top.

Gammon pointed at Nem. "You first."

Nem took the item out of the Exoworlder's hand. The wince in the Boore's eyes was expected. The pain of being healed wasn't nice. What Gammon didn't expect was the Exoworlder saying, "I'll wait here."

"You came all this way to sit outside?" Gammon said, taking the medscope from Nem and gritting his teeth to keep from shouting. Fenock of Fortune that hurt.

"I do not fight."

Gammon grunted. "Yeah, I get that. Your spiked tail and claws are just to scare off predators."

"I do not fight *your* enemy."

Oh.

Nem had already turned back into a black ball of shadow and was headed down into the hole. Gammon followed, using his nose instead of his eyesight to navigate. Thankfully, Nem could see in the dark, so they didn't have to look for the door.

"The door is locked. But there is a crack in the wall. I will go in and open it from the other side," Nem said.

"The Federation is missing out not having Boore under their command."

Nem didn't respond, and Gammon was sure that he had already turned back into a shadow. With a hard bang on the door, it slid open with a creak.

Immediately, Gammon realized that not only had the master changed things on the surface but had shifted things underground, too. The dim lines along the wall's edge showed that the area was far too fancy to be the entrance to a compound.

Lights illuminated the single hallway, and Gammon felt a considerable amount of unease walking down it. The master loved using corridors to disorient his guests and victims.

Nem must have felt it too because he held out his hand. "I will go first."

Gammon watched as Nem turned into a shadow and walked down the hall. Within seconds, sharp wheels with razor-sharp teeth sliced through the air. Nem ran faster until he was past them. Gammon watched carefully, memorizing each area to avoid being sliced open.

As soon as the Boore was through, he clicked his tongue once, giving the all-clear. Gammon took in a breath and held the medscope tightly as he walked down the hall on his toes, making quick jerks to avoid a quick death.

Once he was through, they saw a black door with two red slashes on it. It was the entrance to the stairs that led to the underground. Gammon's blood raced as they got that much closer to the master.

THIRTEEN
THE SON

Amaree understood that the constant explosions were bombs or torpedoes. Not knowing exactly what was going on made her want to scream. The Maw was her cousin's ship, and she figured if he wanted her help, he would ask for it. Still, it gnawed at her to be in this helpless state.

Her heart jumped when the door opened. It calmed when Fenton strolled in. "Hey, you bored?"

"Are you serious?" No, she was freaking out.

Another explosion sounded outside the ship. It rocked the vessel, and Amaree grabbed the counter to anchor herself. When the moment had passed, Fenton pushed off the floor, wiping her backside. "Figures, he'd do that now."

"Who?"

"Your cousin," said Fenton as she waved for Amaree to follow her.

Amaree paused. "Where are we going?"

"In summary, we're going to invade a psychotic Red Demon's mansion, kill any of his pets who try to kill us, and rescue a Kingling."

Uh...

Taking a deep breath, Amaree realized that life on this ship was anything but safe...or normal. Opening a drawer, she picked up four medscopes. "Sounds dangerous. I think medscopes are in order."

"Good thinking," Fenton said.

"Anything else I should know?"

The Ahpaki walked in, holding Amaree's frostic knife. "You might need this," Prussia said, handing the dagger over and grabbing a welding knife from her belt.

Amaree took the weapon, understanding that they believed she might need to use it. In theory, sure. But actually killing someone went against her nature.

"How fast can you get us out of the ship?" Fenton asked.

"The back or the front?"

"Front."

Sliding the knife into the back of her pants, Amaree used her hands to wrap a thin layer of the floor around them, then melted everything else. Amaree had a good idea of the ship's layout, so she moved them diagonally towards the front of the spacecraft.

Once they were outside, she started to retract their protective layer when Kava's voice was suddenly in her head, "*Stay in the ball. There are too many traps along the way. It's not safe.*"

Amaree kept her hands out. "I can't steer if I don't know where I'm going."

"*I'll throw you,*" Kava said.

"Did he just say he would *throw* us?" Fenton said, lowering her body and pressing her hands out to the sides as if preparing to be tossed.

Prussia lowered herself, too. "Hopefully, the landing won't be too painful."

Amaree felt it when Kava's presence wrapped around her protective layer. Her chest squeezed as the sphere jolted forward. It took considerable self-control not to ground the metal, especially when she didn't know where they were going.

"I'm going to catch you, Ree. Have faith."

She did...now.

Taking in a relieved breath, she waited until the ball began to slow and drop. Amaree could feel the connection between the metal and ground the second they touched down. She hesitated for a moment in case Kava told her not to let down her guard.

"Good, you're learning," Kava said.

Keeping the ball solid, she was about to ask what to expect when Kava added, *"I can't hear anyone's voices. They have cerebral blockers on."*

"Then how do you know there are inhabitants here?"

"Mung, the Semp, is on the bridge. He scanned the area with infrared."

Oh. Clever. Wait, "Aren't Semps teleporters?"

"Yes, they are. And, no, he's busy and can't help you."

Oh.

"Mung doesn't see anyone around, but that does not mean you're safe. Keep the metal around you in case you need to shield yourself. Fenton has a map to the master's room. Follow her. When you find the Kingling—Prussia is the only one who can talk to him, so don't try—get back into the sphere, and I'll bring you back."

Amazingly, the plan sounded pretty easy. More confident, she removed the metal from around them. The material was too heavy to hold, and she didn't want it impeding the mission. Thinking fast, she made herself bracers. That didn't take much of the glob, so she made smaller bracelets and fastened them up her arms.

With a small bit left, she made another necklace, this time

drawing it down her back and adding an upside-down sheath for her frostic knife.

Amaree was pleased that she got herself situated before Fenton finished looking over a map on her Minky watch.

"The house is this way." Fenton pointed and began leading the way.

Amaree gave Prussia a jerk of the head to instruct her to go next. It was safer for her to be in the middle. Following behind, she scanned the area, seeing rows of trees lining each side of the stone path. Pale brown sand that moved with each breeze covered the ground.

The path opened, and a massive gold-and-white mansion with a red door and red windows came into view.

The trees and all the greenery were gone. Tall poles with faces carved into them surrounded the house—some sad, others mad, still more happy. One looked to be in agony. The one with the pained face had been painted in browns, black, and green, and stood in the middle of the wide-open area in front of the house. Six male Yunkins with thick red collars were tied to its base. All six moved with a predator's grace, all on alert as if waiting for the perfect time to break out of their collars and run after them.

Amaree slowed, amazed at the inhuman expression they all wore. She cursed under her breath.

"They're feral, don't go near them," Prussia whispered.

Feral was one word to describe them. The animalistic hunger in their eyes said that much. Amaree noticed the hollowed cheeks, the dirty skin, and the emaciated upper bodies, each rib perfectly accentuated. "They're starving," she said, wondering aloud if that was how they ended up looking so savage.

Amaree reached into her pocket and pulled out a medscope. She slowed and got on her knee, tossing the medscope at the closest Yunkin. All six snarled as they rushed to the device. The one she'd tossed it to dug his fingers into the ground to grab it and then opened his mouth, throwing it in. The male must have tried to bite it because his brows pulled together in pain, then he spit it out and let the others fight over the thing.

The male glared at her as if she had tricked him on purpose.

Amaree stood, feeling her heart break. In her mind, she said, "*Kava, we have to save them.*"

"*I saw what they just did through your eyes. Those beasts are not coming on my ship to attack my crew and eat all our food.*"

"*They are being tortured! It's not their fault. Their minds are broken. They need help, not be left to rot.*"

"*You're there for the king's son, not to rescue the planet.*"

Amaree stopped and screamed internally. "*I'M A DOCTOR. Take them to the medical bay and lock the doors. I will pay for whatever they break. Give Mung access to my sight so he can teleport here.*"

"*Ree...*"

"*Kava.*"

"Why have you stopped?" Prussia said.

"We need to save those people," Amaree said, keeping her eyes on the six Yunkins so Mung could come.

"While they stay chained up, they are not our problem," Fenton said as she walked up the front stairs.

With a slight pop, Mung appeared next to Amaree. He looked at her and then at the six Yunkins. Leaning back, he sucked in a breath between his teeth. "This is a bad idea."

"They need help," Amaree admonished.

"They need something," Mung said as he walked to them. The six crouched as if primed to attack. The blue Outworlder's tail stilled as he walked up, just out of their reach, then teleported behind them and took all six away.

Satisfied, Amaree walked up the steps and joined Fenton and Prussia.

With a huff, Fenton said, "This would have been easier if the door was metal." Getting down, she inspected the door as if she were looking for something specific.

Amaree wasn't able to keep up with the quantum search on the Minky watch. But after a minute, the door just popped open.

Fenton turned around and held a finger to her lips. As if they needed to be reminded. Breaking into a house where the owner turns people into animals was scary enough. She definitely didn't want to get caught.

Inside the house, the floors were megal wood, a dark, expensive material with ribbons of gold. The floors, banister, and stairs were all made from megal. The stairs followed the wall up to a considerable height. Amaree figured that if anyone accidentally slipped off the second story, they wouldn't live to reminisce about it.

Fenton looked at her with an expression that said, "*You know what to do,*" but Amaree had no idea. Then Fenton pointed to the floor and flipped her palm up, floating it in the air.

Oh.

Amaree used her ability to lift everyone. Fenton pointed to the stairs and then pulled out two strange-looking guns. They were black with bumps all over them. As they rose, Amaree suddenly stopped when Fenton turned and pulled the trigger on her weapon—or at least she assumed she did.

There was no sound.

Turning, Amaree looked back and saw someone in the process of disappearing. Getting Fenton's attention, she mouthed, "*The hell is that?*"

All Fenton did was shrug and point to the top of the stairs

with the barrel of one of the guns. Amaree tried to move past what she'd seen, but she was seriously confused at a device that could literally disappear someone.

Stepping out from a shadowed section in the wall, a massive Krant wrapped his hand around Fenton's neck. His beady eyes zeroed in on Prussia, and his voice vibrated with authority when he said, "Guess what happens to bad slaves who try and escape."

Prussia brandished her welding knife. "Let her go, and I'll let you live."

The Krant chuckled. "Don't worry, Ahpaki, you're going to be Krant bait, too."

Prussia sliced her weapon up towards the Krant's face. The Krant jerked back and chuckled some more, the sound echoing ominously in the upstairs area.

"Get him in the eyes," Fenton choked out.

Amaree flashed back on Gammon, using her knife to kill a Krant by throwing it through his eye. She didn't want to see that again.

Amaree used her ability to grab everyone and hold them still. Walking to the Krant, she reached up and pulled back each of the thick fingers wrapped around Fenton's neck. When Fenton was free, Amaree turned to Prussia, who kept the welding knife out. "What is Krant bait?"

Before Prussia could answer, Fenton shot the defenseless male in the face without so much as a care. Stunned, Amaree stood there, seeing the mess of meat and blood left behind after the weapon's damage.

"Krant bait is a person who is used for breeding or raping while a Krant is in his two-week breeding haze. Krant women are used to fighting off the men so they can sleep, but in a Krant den, the females can't fight, and they end up dying," Fenton said before shooting the male once more. "And this house slave probably uses Meraderol to induce his mating heat more often."

Meraderol was a Krant medicine to help Krant males produce more sperm so they could have children with their non-Krant mates. The Federation hormone inhibitor sometimes had adverse effects on the Krant's sperm count. But never had Amaree imagined that a male would use it just to go into heat in order to rape another being.

"Let's go," Fenton said before using the gun to make a gesture for Amaree to lift them back into the air.

Amaree did as directed and floated them towards where Fenton pointed her weapon. A room with two tall doors was at the back of the wall, the panels gold with a red symbol of what could be a face but one wider than it was tall. Its mouth was bent down, and it was uncomfortable to look at.

Fenton pulled up her Minky watch and once more searched for something. About a minute later, the door snicked and then opened.

Inside, the room smelled different than the cleaning solution clearly used in the house. It smelled like candles, oil, leather, and ash. Amaree didn't know where it was located, but a fireplace was lit somewhere in the room.

The floors were no longer wood but black-and-gold stone. Soft, red fabric covered the walls. From where she stood, Amaree could see no windows. The only illumination came from the half-dome lights in the vaulted ceiling.

Setting everyone down, Fenton made a hand motion for them to search the place. Fenton turned left and headed down a hall, and Amaree took the right corridor. It emptied into a large entertainment room with a long table, chairs, and place settings. Stepping into the room, the door slammed shut, and another Krant reached out to grab Amaree.

Holding her hands up, she froze him. His eyes widened for

a moment, but then they narrowed as if he were pissed that she was defending herself. Grabbing a vambrace from her wrist, she looked at the male and hesitated with what she needed to do.

Using her added ability, she struck him over the temple and saw the light go out in his eyes. Setting him down on the floor, she didn't bother checking for a pulse at his neck. The skin was too thick. Pulling down his bottom lip, she checked the vein that ran through his mouth to ensure it had not darkened to indicate he was losing oxygen to his blood.

Seeing that it was the perfect color, she let him go and stepped over him. The door was locked, but it was thankfully metal, so she walked through it. For some reason, the hall looked different, and she felt as if she was going the wrong way. Backing up to the entertainment room door, she held her hand to the wall. Under the fabric was metal. But past that was wood. Using the metal wall, she bent it with one hard mental push and broke the wood so she could squeeze back into the right hall. As she stepped through, she got a head rush, and her vision got spotty.

Ignoring the feeling, she walked back down the hall, taking deep breaths to help dispel whatever was wrong with her.

Back at the front of the room, she saw Prussia in the same spot. Fenton's cheek was red, and Amaree wondered what she'd found...or what had found her. But more, she wondered what they were looking at.

At the front of the room were three black scaly-looking décor chairs. Amaree was about to ask the females what was wrong when she saw Fenton pointing to the first chair.

Amaree walked over and saw the seat move. The small shift gave her a better sightline to what they were looking at. It was a curled-up black Kingling. His ear had moved because he heard her coming closer.

Peering at Fenton, Amaree tried to ask if she should put them into a ball again.

Fenton shook her head once.

Amaree squatted down, hoping to determine if he needed medical assistance, when Prussia pulled a strand of her hair. Grabbing her head, Amaree looked back at the Ahpaki with a glare.

"*Don't touch him,*" she mouthed.

"*I'm not,*" she mouthed back.

Using hand gestures, Prussia instructed Amaree to move out of the way. As soon as she was up, Prussia moved to the other side and blew out a breath from between her lips. Not a whistle and barely loud enough to hear, but the curled-up male instantly unfurled his head. The Kingling male pointed his nose at her and silently sniffed the air. Prussia pulled something out of her pocket and laid it in front of him and then moved back. Without even looking at the offering, the Kingling tucked himself into a ball and closed his eyes, making it difficult to see anything but scales.

Amaree blinked back tears. If the Kingling was an animal, it would have been the best-trained animal in the universes. But this was a person, and someone had turned him into a pet—a docile and obedient beast.

What disturbed her more was that Kinglings were absolute savages, a race that feared nothing and lived to fight for fun and money.

Amaree's father and mother had taken her to meet a yellow Kingling named Moddoe. He lived in a big tent on a dry planet. She remembered that he and a younger Kingling her size had been playing. The young one had tried to get her to play-fight. The younger one slapped her with his sword, not cutting but irritating her. Once he got close to actually cutting her so she pushed him back with her telekinesis and held him down on his back as she scolded him in the only way a three-year-old girl could.

She didn't remember what had caused her father and mother to scoop her up so fast and leave the planet, but she *did* remember that her father had told her that Kinglings were dangerous, and that she should stay away from them.

Looking at the curled-up Kingling on the ground, he looked harmless. Not someone who was potentially dangerous and simply refrained from hurting others, but absolutely defenseless.

Prussia made another sound. A quick click-click with her tongue.

The Kingling hissed but didn't move.

Prussia looked at Amaree and Fenton, her brows furrowed. Fenton tapped her watch, and Prussia nodded. Pushing to her knees, she pulled off her belt and wrapped it around the Kingling's neck.

Prussia stood and tugged, and the male moved...just as a pet would. The look on the Ahpaki's face said more than Amaree could translate. But, instinctively, she understood.

A loud bang echoed in the house, and Fenton snapped her fingers and circled them in the air. Amaree pulled out all the metal and wrapped them completely, feeling lightheaded again.

The black Kingling cowered and curled up into a ball. In the process of doing that, he had ripped the belt away from Prussia, scraping her skin. Amaree knew this because she smelled the female's blood. It wasn't a deep wound, and she would fix it later.

Lifting the ball to the ceiling, she was grateful when she felt the honed vibration of the metal. Melting through it, she hoped that Kava would be able to steer them once she was out. Just as she hoped, the moment they were past the roof, she felt Kava's presence grabbing the sphere.

"You're crashing, Ree. I need you to hold it together."

Fighting the Cerebral overload, she took in a slow breath and focused. Lives were at stake.

To her left, she heard a high-pitched whistle. She barely had time to register the noise before feeling the heat and separation of the metallic elements. A bright light swept over her, and then she immediately dropped from the air.

FOURTEEN
THE TRAINING CAGES

The stairs were pitch-black. Gammon could smell his brother-in-arms, but he couldn't see him. Unease filled him, not knowing if the master had put death traps on the stairway. He jerked to a stop when he didn't find the next step but solid ground.

The smell of various races, blood, vomit, and decay had not changed since he was in this underground hell last time. He was about to shout out for Nem, but the lights flickered on, row by row.

A straight line of them from one side of the space to the other. The light farthest back illuminated first. The raised platform for the training fights brought back so many bad memories for Gammon. Being whipped with the electric flogger and having his skin shredded open.

The next section to light was the washing room, which was empty. The rusted pipes weren't even dripping water.

The next section was the cages, and that extended for at least one hundred yards. Gammon watched with a mixture of fear, anger, and wrath as each cage stood open as if freedom was so close. Yet each being stood in fighting leathers, each in the middle of their wire prisons, staring at Gammon with predatory intent.

Each one wore a collar with a blinking red light.

Gammon knew exactly what it was like to wear something that directed every single moment of your life. When you moved, when you ate, slept, and even defecated. The red light meant that no one moved or an electric current would slice through you—and could kill you.

Back at the training platform, the master rose from the steps, moving to the middle. His hair was gone, and his face looked thin and saggy. But even from the great distance, Gammon knew his scent.

The Red Demon wore his long, black cloak. The same one he wore when he attended the fights. When he dipped his head in the way he did when assessing someone else's fighter, Gammon's spine straightened.

"You've gotten fat, Gammon. And fat fighters are too slow to win against my pets," the master called out but immediately started to cough. Suddenly, the master jerked with a hiss as if he were angry that his body was breaking down.

The Red Demon pulled up his sleeve, and once again, Gammon was surprised by the lack of thickness. The master, for all the hundreds of years Gammon had known him, had been solid as stone with thick, black hair and wiry, strength-filled limbs. The muscles were always so clearly defined.

They weren't now.

The male before Gammon was dying.

Gammon was thankful that he was able to be here, to do what he was about to do. To ensure the master didn't spend days or months on his deathbed, reliving all that he had accomplished. All the lives he'd destroyed—with glee.

"As a Demon, I'm in the mood to offer you a deal. If you can make it past my pets, I'll fight you. One-on-one. If you win, you can leave with your life. If not, then my pets will eat you."

Gammon felt something brush the back of his neck, making his hair rise. At first, Gammon wondered if another Boore was behind him, one that would take him down and deliver him to the master.

The faint growl, though, he recognized as Nem, and Gammon almost smiled at the sound of the Boore's impatience.

Taking in a lungful of air, Gammon called back, "It's a deal, you limp-faced bastard."

The Red Demon stared as if he didn't understand the insult, then his upper lip curled, and he snorted. "You're dead, Gammon."

Pulling a device from beneath the cloak, the master pushed something to make all the collars turn green. "The one who brings me the first body part will feast from my table for a year."

The fighters moved like lightning, dead looks in their eyes as various males of various races moved like a raging river. Gammon sprinted for the first cage to get the higher ground.

Five fighters surrounded him, throwing deadly hits that Gammon barely had time to block. Nem's shadow tore one down by snapping his neck, and the two nearest to that one hesitated—

Giving Gammon an opening to throat-punch one and leap for the cage. He felt the jabs in his back from the fighters, but if he gave up, he would absolutely die. With a few direct kicks—and Nem's help—Gammon made it to the top.

The fighters surrounded him, but kicking faces in wasn't hard, and it gave the medscope time to heal his internal wounds.

The cages were situated close enough together that Gammon leapt from one to the next before other fighters figured it out and climbed up onto all the cages surrounding him, effectively blocking him from the master.

Gammon picked the one who would get him closer to the platform and jumped. The fighter was a Night Demon with knuckles that had pointed, three-inch bones sticking out of them.

The emaciated male moved faster than Gammon and got him in the face. The sting burned but didn't stop Gammon from kicking out and jerking back. The Night Demon threw punch after punch in endless combinations that made Gammon's eyes blur.

When the Demon scored a deep punch to Gammon's arm, chest, and stomach, Gammon grabbed the hand, fell back, and kicked the bastard's shoulder, knocking him over and ripping the arm from the socket, shredding anything that held it together.

The Demon roared. Instead of twisting the arm completely off and taking a bite out of it like he would if the male weren't a slave pet, Gammon instead knocked him off the cage and jumped onto the next.

The next fighter was a Yunkin with soulless eyes. Gammon had met plenty of Yunkins who ended up mentally broken from the cages. They didn't speak, didn't know their names, and they only knew how to fight.

This one did what they all did: he charged, and Gammon quickly took the hit around the waist so he could use his elbow and drive it deeply into the top of the spine, killing the slave quickly.

The body slumped, and Gammon jumped again, taking out the next fighter before jumping from the cage to the platform. Holding out his hands, he shook them. "A deal's a deal."

Rising with an electric whip in one hand, the Red Demon stood, unafraid and smirking.

"You brought your own pet, I see. A Boore, given the black

shadow I saw moving between my pets. I can't wait to meet him and make him mine." He snickered.

A part of Gammon wanted to let the Demon know who it was, but knowing would only give the master more of an advantage in the verbal sparring department.

"Kneel, and beg me to spare your life," the male hissed.

By all that was holy. There was that pain in his gut. Old conditions from before rearing their ugly heads and reminding him that he would suffer greatly if he didn't kneel.

The master pulled out an ear-piercing clicker. Gammon realized that he had waited too long. He should have rushed the Demon when he had the chance.

Nem's shadow did exactly that as the bastard clicked the thing. It shot out a high-pitched, warbling electronic noise that made hearing, seeing, and standing virtually impossible. Nem's shadow dropped to the ground, frozen, and the Boore curled into a ball as he held his ears.

Every other fighter around the platform did, too.

Gammon, however, stayed upright, even though the pain in his ears was serious. If he didn't have the medscope, he doubted that he would be standing as he was. The noise had dropped him the first—and the millionth—time he'd fought against the master. It was the one thing that ended all fights.

Seeing his brother-in-arms starting to shake and scream jolted Gammon from his spot and thrust him forward. He had to finish the master—and fast. He moved towards the Demon, hands loose and rocking on the balls of his feet.

The red bastard snarled as he reached back for his whip. "I will teach you to attack your master!"

Gammon used his fist to take the first snap of the whip. Then he used the half-second of free time to grab the Demon's face and bite it, spitting out the foulness of the flesh.

The electric whip got him before he could do more.

Another hit sliced him down the torso, but again, the medscope gave him enough protection to roll over, open his mouth and sink his teeth into bony and sinewy flesh.

The Demon snarled, and Gammon felt the master's fist slam down on his temple. Dazed, Gammon rolled back and scissor-kicked the male's knee. Another slice of the whip came down and opened Gammon's face.

Blood coated his mouth, but he didn't feel anything but pleasure as he finally saw fear in his old master's eyes. "What kind of cybernetic trick is this?"

Gammon didn't respond as he launched himself at the Demon again. He wrapped his arms around the master and got him into a three-point hold. The high-pitched echo stopped, but the ringing in his head had not abated.

Twisting with increased pressure, the Demon scratched and fought the chokehold.

Then, like a reaper rising from the grave, Nem rose slowly, his red eyes blazing, brandishing his thick, pointed teeth. With perfect accuracy, the Boore punched through the Demon's rib cage. The body jerked and shook.

Nem withdrew the master's heart, and Gammon got to feel the moment when the body sagged, instantly lifeless.

Waiting to see if Nem ate the organ, Gammon held his breath and the dead master's head.

Sniffing the bloody organ, Nem said, "This is rotten."

Sniffing the air, Gammon was surprised to realize that it truly *did* smell rotten. It even looked shriveled.

Nem held up the heart and let out a victory roar.

Gammon dropped the body and scanned the pets who stared at Nem, most unmoving and unsure. Turning back around, Gammon rifled through the dead male's pockets, found the master remote for the collars, and pointed it at the slaves. Using his commander tone, he told them, "I'm Commander

Gammon of the Federation. As of this moment, you no longer serve a master." He clicked the release button and saw the green lights turn off.

It took a few more seconds for the more intelligent pets to take off their collars. Then, the rest followed suit. Gammon broke the device as he added, "A red ship waits on the landing pad. Food, water, and medical supplies will be available to you."

Considering this was a Federation mission, all the survivors would need to be taken to the ship and entered into the archives. From there, his poor mate would have to do hundreds of medical assessments.

Gammon knew that some of the slaves were more alert and aware of themselves. The others would need a great deal of therapy and rehabilitation. Not being a doctor, he didn't know the protocol for all of it, but he *did* know that everyone would get the help they needed.

"FOOD," a male bellowed, and the majority of the males ran, pushing and growling as they rushed around the platform towards the stairs that led to the upper story.

"Not that way," Gammon yelled, but the stampede of people was single-mindedly focused. Addressing Nem, he asked, "Can you follow them and make sure they make it back to the ship? We can't leave them here. The Federation will take them in and help them."

Nem growled as if he'd rather not but faded into a shadow and jumped off the platform, weaving his way through the crowd.

Out of the hundreds, fifty or so remained still. All of them were Night or Roth Demons. Not one Terran, Yunkin, Bolark, Sennite, Grach, or Hetten in the bunch. With almost a hundred years in the Federation, Gammon understood that Demons were stubborn bastards.

The same Night Demon he'd fought earlier, moved to the

base of the stairs. "You were a pet before the Federation or after?"

"After."

"Really?" the Demon snorted. "When did the Federation move into the Outworlds?"

"What's your name?" Gammon asked.

The Demon hesitated. "Qraw."

"Well, Qraw, they're not the controlling force, but they're doing what they can to climb the ladder."

Qraw nodded. "Taking out the master was a smart move."

Gammon didn't know if Qraw had experience in the Federation or if he was a Demon dealer. Either way, it was time to leave.

"What are you planning to do with us? Considering most of us are killers, I doubt the Federation will let us cross the borders."

Gammon pointed to the stairway he'd come from. "First thing I'm going to do is lead you back to the ship. After that, you'll need a shower and food. After *that*, the admiral will decide."

"I've got a better idea. You take us back to your ship. We'll shower, eat, and take the free ride off this planet. But your admiral doesn't need to know about us or dictate where we go. In return, we'll watch over the feral beasts that would try to eat all your food and kill everyone on the ship."

Qraw was a dealer.

Kava's voice was quick to enter into his mind. "*Tell the bastard I said the feral pets will stay in the brig. He and his Demons can stay in the Level-2 cabins until we drop them off at Port Nicca. It's the only open port available. Also, if he or any of his men disrespects my crew in any way, I will kill them. And no one will know because they don't want to be added to the Federation mission notes.*"

Gammon cleared his throat and relayed the message.

Qraw leaned back, and with uncertainty in his tone, said, "Interesting threat from a Federation captain."

"I'm Federation, not the captain."

"Who's the captain of the red ship?"

"Kava."

"Of the Maw?" the Demon asked, surprised.

Gammon nodded.

Qraw turned and held out an arm as if saying, "*Lead the way.*"

FIFTEEN
BECOMING A PIRATE

Amaree couldn't see or catch anyone in her group before crashing to the ground, feet-first and landing hard on her side. Her ankle throbbed, her head ached, and her muscles were sore as she rolled up, grabbed the first medscope she got her hands on and crawled on the soft dune to the closest person.

She placed the medscope on Prussia's chest, just as a crazy-looking Terran came running towards her at full-speed. He had a mallet in his hand or something non-metallic and led the attack with at least ten other males.

Amaree tried to connect to the humans and toss them back, but her Cerebral abilities didn't register anything.

She cursed as she grabbed her frostic knife, but then the Terran's eyes widened all of a sudden, seconds before all their heads fell off. It was like an invisible knife had cut them all from their shoulders.

The bodies toppled over. Amaree felt Kava as he made her turn her head to scan the area.

Amaree did so, giving in to her cousin's control as she looked for Fenton. That's the need Kava fed her. His need and desperation to find Fenton—his mate.

The black Kingling lay near the top of the dune, so she scrambled over, moving easier now after the medscope's wonderful healing abilities.

Another wild-eyed male was there, knife in hand. He had already stabbed the Kingling and was raising his weapon for another slice. Amaree didn't think; she just pulled out her frostic blade and thrust it between the male's ribs, directly into his heart. Righteous anger consumed her as she seethed at the bastard who would dare attack the most helpless creature/being in all the 'verses.

Placing the second medscope on the Kingling, Amaree prayed to Seth of Stars that the scopes were programmed for the race. If not, she had to get him back to the medical bay because he wasn't moving.

Kinglings hadn't been part of her medical training, so she did not know if his heart had stopped, or even if there was a specific place to find it. Checking the blood, she could only see one wound, and it was on the back left shoulder.

She palpated the area around the wound to see if she could find the point of impact, but she couldn't see it. Still, the small, shuddering breath from the male let her know that he was alive.

Thankfully.

Another war cry sounded from somewhere behind her, and she turned to see Prussia fighting off one Sennite male. Another Yunkin was coming over the dune. In complete emergency mode, Amaree focused on the attackers and hoped that she didn't have to ask Kava to do what he had before.

A heartbeat later, both males lost their heads. Calling down to Prussia, she said, "The son's up here."

Prussia quickly moved up the dune, and Amaree instructed her, "I think the wound has healed, but there is a ton of sand out here, so it will need to be re-opened and cleaned. I also want to make sure that nothing else happened during the fall, but I can't do that now. We need to get him back to the ship."

"I'll take him," Prussia said, digging a hand under the sand and lifting him onto her shoulder.

The male's eyes opened for a second and then closed again. Amaree had no idea what that meant. She also didn't want Prussia thinking she was alone. "Keep your eyes open. Kava can see through your vision, and he will make sure no one touches you. Okay?"

"I know my captain watches over us," Prussia said, beginning to walk down the dune. A second later, the blue Semp popped up next to her, wrapped a hand around both of them, and then all three were gone.

Standing up, Amaree didn't see anything or anyone until a round trap door opened, and another wild male, this one a Bolark, scrambled out and over to the base of the two dunes.

Amaree was already running forward to see what he had found. A piece of flat metal lay on the ground, and it took the Bolark throwing off the cover before she saw Fenton's body, lying unnaturally still with half her form burned and blackened.

Kava's roar echoed in Amaree's mind and in the air. A charge of electricity pricked at Amaree's skin as she rushed to Fenton's body, praying that Kava didn't do something stupid like pick her up and take her back to the ship.

Just as she thought that, she was lifted off the sand and flung to Fenton's side. The Bolark saw her and pulled out a knife, but Amaree's frostic blade was already pushing into his chest, straight to the heart, ending his life quickly.

Checking for a pulse, she pulled out the third medscope and placed it on Fenton's burned face. There was no pulse, but Amaree knew that as soon as her heart started beating and her wounds scabbed over, Fenton would hate her because each wound would have to be re-opened, cleaned, and checked.

"Come on, come on, come on," Amaree pleaded. The blue Semp appeared with a pop, and Amaree held up a finger, needing him to wait. Just as she'd hoped, Fenton gasped for breath, and Amaree could feel the weak pulse getting stronger under her fingers.

"Now, may I?" the Semp asked.

Amaree backed up to let the male take her, but he reached out with his tail and wrapped it around her wrist. "We go together," he said. With a strange, tingling feeling, she closed her eyes and then opened them again to find herself inside the medical bay.

As soon as the Semp's tail let her go, she remembered something. "Wait, my frostic knife is still in the Bolark."

The male eyed her. "I save people, not knives."

"Please, it's frostic," she said, knowing he didn't understand why it was so valuable to her.

He rolled his eyes and teleported away. Fenton was awake and trying to sit up, but Amaree tapped her shoulder and told her, "You're not going to like it, but I need to re-open all your wounds and clean them out so they can heal properly."

"Not in your life, witch. I have a mate lecturing me about never going on another mission again, and a king to get a hold of." Fenton tried to move again, and Amaree held her down.

Fenton's face shut down and got serious. "Let me up, or you and I will have problems."

The Semp popped in just then, and Amaree took that second to inject Fenton with a non-sleep paralysis medication. Fenton's body went limp, and there was little doubt that Fenton would seek vengeance when this was all over.

The Semp put down the frostic knife and left. Amaree felt a thousand percent more focused and in charge as she moved on autopilot, taking the scans, removing the clothes in the affected areas, and cutting the flesh to the bone while probably freaking

Fenton out, but Fenton was...a pirate. A killer. And if seeing her own bones freaked her out, well...tough luck.

After finishing her task, she healed the female. Most of Fenton's left side had to be re-grown, but no one would be able to tell. As soon as it was done, Amaree pulled out an antidote and returned Fenton's control of her faculties. The female sat up on the medical slab and pointed a finger.

But every time Fenton was about to say something, she stalled. Finally, she said, "If you ever do that again...you better knock me out. I never want to see you pulling my body apart in front of me again."

Amaree nodded. "That's fair."

Fenton shivered. "I'm going to have nightmares."

Amaree was put off by that. "How can you have nightmares when you've killed so many people?" Of course, Amaree was well aware that she was a hypocrite because she'd killed people too. But at least she felt bad about it. Well...*now* she did. Not so much when it happened.

Fenton sobered, but before saying anything, the medical door opened, and Kava walked in. The two walked toward each other and embraced in a way that meant even Amaree could see the high and volatile emotions soothing.

The door opened again, and clothes floated in the air. Fenton must have seen them because she chuckled and whispered something to Kava that Amaree couldn't hear. Then, she took the clothes and went into the extra medical room.

Kava wiped his face and whispered, "Thank you for saving her, but please don't let her watch next time. I was there, too, experiencing it with her, and I never want to see that again either."

"I've already promised I wouldn't," Amaree said as her mind flashed back to a few moments from when they invaded the big, white house. Pushing those uncomfortable images away, she remembered the slaves she'd asked the Semp to rescue. "Where are the six Yunkins?"

"In the brig," Kava said, looking towards the room Fenton had gone into.

She'd told him to put them in medical, but she understood keeping them from hurting anyone on the ship. Still, considering their mental and medical state, she felt bad for them. Worse when she thought of the other mindless males she'd killed.

"Where's that? I need to get them. They're just responding to being starved. Once they get some food, a hot shower, some clean clothes, and a medical once-over, they should get a little better."

Kava shook his head. "Those Yunkins are trained killers."

Amaree frowned. "I don't understand what you mean. Are you saying they were Federation soldiers?"

"I don't know if they were ever in the Federation. Their thoughts never went there, but I do know that a Demon who made a living out of training people to be pets mentally broke them."

"Pets?" Amaree repeated, knowing that what he said was true because the Kingling acted just like a pet. Still, the thought was too inhumane. She tried not to count how many wild males had attacked her, but she couldn't help it. "Why would anyone do that?"

Kava just looked at her, knowing that she knew why but she didn't want to think about it. Being a doctor, she did know. Some people were messed up emotionally, mentally, and physically. Sometimes, it was the situations they were born into. Other times, it was just who the person was.

Someone who made people into pets was a monster, and Amaree hoped that Kava had taken care of him.

Kava watched as the door opened, and Fenton walked out.

He didn't say anything until he had wrapped Fenton in his arms and had lifted them into the air, floating out of the medical bay.

"The Red Demon who systematically broke hundreds if not thousands of people was not killed by me but by Gammon and Nem. They were once his pets, and they were due the right to take his life."

Amaree's eyes closed as she dropped into the nearest chair. Gammon had been one of the pets? No wonder he turned cannibal when starved. Being one of the emaciated, chained pets would have done that to him.

"Gammon and Nem were what the Demon called fighting slaves. They were trained and used as fighters against anyone and anything. The fights were to the death, and whoever won, was given the dead body to eat as a reward."

Amaree curled over until her elbows rested on her thighs. She couldn't imagine how awful that must have been to be reduced to an animal state like that. She couldn't imagine how Gammon probably spent every day, wishing he was free. Then, when he escaped, he joined the Federation only for a backstabbing Sennite to ruin his life again and be kidnapped by a horrible pirate who treated him as an animal. Again. *Then,* he had the misfortune of meeting her, someone who'd mated him and then tried to *break it.*

It was amazing he could even look at her.

"I need to be with my mate right now so this is my last comment, Ree. Don't mistake Gammon for a broken pet. He's not. He escaped and joined the Federation as a Grach, which means he spent seventy-five years at the academy and the next hundred climbing the ranks to become a commander. He is not trying to fill an emotional hole. He's doing what his people do. He found his mate, he mated her, and now he will spend the rest of his life with you. No matter where you are or what job you take, he will be with you, and he will be at peace."

Hearing that didn't make Amaree feel better, but then it suddenly did because at least Gammon didn't regret choosing her.

Sitting up, she looked at the door and wondered when he would be back. She wondered if he was in pain and suffering, or if he would need—and accept—her help. A part of her wanted to stay in her seat and wait until he returned. But then she remembered the Kingling and knew she needed to check on him.

The problem was, she knew that Kava wasn't listening to her anymore, and she had no idea where Prussia had taken the king's son. Sitting back, she took a deep, irritated breath. As she did, she realized that she smelled more than just Fenton and Kava. She could also smell the Semp and melted fabric.

Taking another deep breath, she smelled a hint of soap and realized that Fenton didn't just change, she'd showered, too.

Closing her eyes, Amaree inhaled again and removed all the scents she'd already identified to find that her knife had the smell of musk and ash. The other scent was too unique, and she couldn't identify it.

Opening her eyes, she sniffed around and realized that it came from the blade of her weapon. The bad smells were coming from there.

"So, I inherited his sense of smell, too." Interesting.

Taking a handful of things she guessed she might need, she left the medical bay and took the elevator door. Once she was down, she closed her eyes and thought about the Kingling. She inhaled slowly and deeply.

There.

She remembered his smell. Following the traces in the air, she went to treat her most-sensitive patient. When she was finished with him, she would figure out what to do about the Yunkins.

SIXTEEN

A PIRATE WITH TOO MUCH POWER

The walk back took longer than he wanted. The fifty-six Demons and two hundred and forty-one feral bastards acted more like wild prey. They kept trying to break through the line of Demons. To keep them from being herded to the ship.

Nem had caught up to the idiot leader and scared them all back down to the cages, where they rejoined Gammon.

The winged Exoworlder had filled the black lake with enough bones that everyone could cross safely. When everyone was safely over the tar, Antonis left them to return on their own.

Gammon wasn't surprised to see the dunes that surrounded the landing pad flattened and black. Millions of pieces of shrapnel littered the landing pad. What did surprise him was that there wasn't a single scratch, dent, or burn mark on the Maw's red paint.

Kava, the Cerebral, stood at the foot of the ramp as if waiting for them. And maybe he was, because every single feral bastard was lifted up into the air and funneled into the ship through the small opening.

Yellow eyes scanned the rest of the males. He lingered on some as if reading their minds and sizing everyone up. If

Gammon were one of the survivors, he would have been pretty damn intimidated.

Interestingly enough, Gammon was close enough to hear Qraw tell another Night Demon, "Well, that was terrifying."

Kava didn't say anything to the fighters who passed him. All of them dropped their gazes, and Gammon knew that even though they looked and talked like someone not affected by the master's mental conditioning, they proved the lie of that right then by treating Kava like they had the master.

Nem waited until all the slaves were headed up the ramp before he bowed his head, "Thank you, Captain."

Kava nodded. "Good fighting, Nem."

Nem hesitated as if he might say something else, but he didn't. A moment later, he headed up the ramp.

Gammon wouldn't call Kava "*Captain,*" but he did say, "Thanks for your help."

Kava smirked.

Jerk.

"Looks like we have one more thing to do, and then it's over. You get your ship back, and I get to retire. A win-win."

"Can't get going on that last thing while you're standing here."

Gammon snorted at Kava's comment. It wasn't said with enough disdain for him to believe that Kava was counting down the seconds until the mission was over.

Antonis flew out of the ship and landed hard, or maybe it was just his tail that landed hard. The spikes weren't bone. "Fenton says we are leaving now."

"I know," Kava said.

Antonis hesitated as he scanned the damage around the ship. His jaw flexed before he said, "This planet is cursed."

Gammon cleared his throat. "It's not a vacation spot, that's for sure."

Antonis looked confused for a moment, and then asked Kava, "Will you give them rest?"

"Who?" Gammon said, wondering if the winged male was talking about the dead. At the same time, Kava said, "Yes."

Yes?

"Who are you... What are you going to do?" Gammon asked.

"Are there any more slaves on the planet?"

"Slaves? No."

"I'm sure some of the master's workers are still on the planet," Gammon said.

"They are not slaves, and their deaths will please the dead."

Kava looked at Gammon as if to say, "*See? Now shut up and get on the ship.*"

Antonis snapped out his wings and flew back up the ramp and onto the ship.

Kava headed towards the black dunes, and Gammon couldn't help but question him again. "What are you doing?"

Kava flicked his fingers, and Gammon was lifted off the ground and floated to the edge of the ramp. Gammon wished there was a floating blocker. Something to keep from being picked up and moved around like a human balloon all the time.

Kava stopped well before the dunes and pressed a single hand against the dirt. Gammon didn't see anything happen, but the foul stench of ozone congested the air. Amaree smelled the same when she used her Cerebral abilities.

An unnatural sound rumbled from deep beneath the surface, and Gammon had to stick his head outside to verify that the sound was indeed coming from the ground. A snap echoed all around him, and his skin felt as if millions of pricks of micro-lightning landed on him.

Then the ground shook, and Gammon fell to his knees, just as the ground broke apart ten yards from where the ship sat.

Kava stood up and walked back to the spacecraft, his face long and eyelids drooped. Gammon noticed that his skin was grey, not its usual color. Maybe using his powers to unsettle the tectonic plates of the planet or whatever it was that he'd done had caused him to overuse his power.

Just as Kava reached the top of the ramp and looked out at the horizon, the dunes looked as if they were sinking.

Another rumble and crack sounded, and Gammon was struck dumb as the ground a few hundred yards out simply...fell. "What was that?"

Kava didn't answer as he sluggishly walked past.

Gammon hit the button to pull up the ramp and followed the Cerebral. As stupid as it was, he asked again, "What did you do?"

"I destroyed the planet," Kava whispered.

Gammon thought that's what had happened, but to actually see it was another thing. Something heavy settled in his chest. The male in front of him was the most dangerous being alive.

No one could keep him in check. No one could challenge him and win. The only thing keeping the Cerebral from taking over and crowning himself a god was...himself.

Unable to process the immensity of that, Gammon followed Kava to the elevator. Standing there, the male whispered, "Fenton."

Gammon didn't understand if Kava was calling his mate or if the Cerebral were telling Gammon to get her.

"No, you paranoid old man. Fenton is what keeps me...me."

Oh.

Yes.

Being mated *would* have affected him, but Gammon had not thought it was that deep. With the Cerebral's abilities, he didn't think anyone could truly control him.

"I wish you had a cerebral blocker, Gammon. Your thoughts are annoying."

The elevator opened, and they both stepped in. "I'll see if Amaree has one in the medical bay," he said as the cab rose, but the hum of the ship did, too, letting him know that the spacecraft was taking off, as well.

Kava closed his eyes and let his head drop back. He looked truly exhausted. But not enough that he would stumble or fall down. "Stop thinking or I will kill you. I won't even feel bad when I lie to my cousin and say that you died on the planet."

The bastard would.

Gammon got off on the medical floor, about to respond, when he saw five Yunkins lined up near the wall, and Antonis standing guard.

The five Yunkins were spread out, each protecting a cooking sheet with barbecued tamin and several bags of water. Each one eating fast as they eyed the others. They kept moving nervously in the hall, keeping tabs on each other.

Peering back at the elevator, Gammon thought about telling Kava that gassing them in the brig would make their checkups go faster, but the elevator was closed, and Gammon heard the sound of the Yunkins' hissing followed by slapping sounds and a metal twang.

Antonis pulled them apart. "Eat your own food."

Another Yunkin with the master's mark licked his sheet and noticed Gammon. Picking up the tray and claiming ownership, the male hissed. Gammon internally shook his head, knowing the Yunkins would need to be sent to the brig after their medical checks.

Before entering the bay, he gave the withered Yunkin a snarl.

Inside, he smelled his mate and another Yunkin. The heat of aggression bubbled up inside him at seeing the male lying on the medical slab. There was a *male* inside his territory. And his territory had morphed from a cabin to everywhere his mate was.

Amaree was on a Minky screen, talking to another male, but Gammon's possessiveness waned when he noticed the male's yellow eyes and a bone structure similar to the Maw's captain.

Gammon didn't think twice about interrupting the call, but halfway to the slab, he heard Amaree sniff the air and whip around. Her eyes found him, and his body stalled, amazed that she seemed to know his scent and responded instantly.

Amaree's beautiful green-blue eyes went from strained to relieved. She bit her lip, and he could smell all the simmering feelings she had. Sure of what he needed to do, he strode over, grabbed her neck, and pressed his head to hers. He would have kissed her, but if he started that, he wouldn't stop.

"Can I help?" he asked.

He could practically smell the unshed tears as she sucked in a breath. "Thank you. Can you take this one to a cabin?"

No. But he'd take him to a cell in the brig. "Okay."

"Do you have any injuries?"

Letting go, he pulled out his medscope. "I'm perfectly healthy."

"You smell like blood. There are clean clothes in the extra medical room," she said in a voice that was stronger than before. Leaning back, he looked at her face and noticed a dramatic change. She was steady, confident, and her eyes were alert.

Knowing that his presence gave her that made something swell inside him, and he felt like he could have commanded an empire with that feeling. Then she lifted her chin and made a trilling sound in her throat, and good Fenock, he was undone.

Gutted.

Grounded.

Loved.

He brushed her lips with his, practically tasting his home, his haven—and trilled back.

"I'm gonna go. Jandy just got home. If she sees you...with *that,* I'm sure I'll get blamed for something, especially since my son hasn't told anyone that you're helping him or that you're seeing someone."

"She's mated," Gammon said, loud enough the male could hear.

Amaree winced.

The male on the call said, "Even worse."

The hum of the call ended, and Gammon knew the other party terminated it. He didn't care that Amaree's family might not understand, but he didn't like the wince she gave. Before he could address that, she said, "Even though I'm an adult with my own career, my parents may not like that I'm mated. So, I'm sorry in advance for what they will say."

"No matter what your parents say, I'm never giving you up. You're mine."

"I know," she said with a glimmer in her eye.

"Do you?" he asked, needing to hear the confirmation.

"Yes. I chose you, remember? If I didn't, we wouldn't be mated."

Damn, he really wished she wasn't busy with over two hundred slaves to scan and attend to. He wanted nothing more than to reward that comment with hours of pleasure and smothering her skin with his scent.

Unfortunately, work came first. But if he could speed it up, he would. "Rotating five pets out of the hundreds will take a long time. Are you sure you want to do it that way?"

"What do you mean, hundreds?"

What did he mean? Pointing to the Yunkin on the slab, he said, "He's a slave from the brig, correct? And you're doing the scans for the mission notes, right?"

"No," she said slowly. "I didn't know there were more on the ship. When did that happen?"

"How many do you think we rescued?"

"*I* rescued six that were chained to a pole in front of a massive white house."

Gammon looked back down at the *guard dog* who had stopped struggling. His eyes said he was paying attention.

Guard dogs were just as bad as fighters, but they had different training. Gammon was trained to fight bigger, stronger opponents and kill with the least amount of energy.

Guard dogs were trained to snap to attention and run down an escaped slave—day or night. They were also encouraged to kill in the most painful ways possible. Just thinking about Amaree saving one...wait a damn minute!

"How did you know they were chained up to the pole?"

"I saw them."

She was being vague on purpose. He could smell her anxiety. "Through a Minky screen?"

"No," she said, getting a little defensive.

"You left the ship?" he asked, knowing that his voice was rising.

"I helped Fenton get the Kingling."

She'd helped Fenton get the Kingling? As in, she'd left the ship, got close enough to a pack of guard dogs to want to save them, and at some point, entered the house—the bloody place of nightmares and hidden hallways.

He felt his hand twitch, clenching into a fist. Gammon was cycling through a lot of emotions, too many to stop him from seething, "Have you lost your damn mind? What in the hell made you act so stupid?"

Her brows pulled together, and she leaned back. He smelled the hurt and the anger, but that didn't stop him because he was angrier and more terrified. "Do you have any idea what could have happened to you? You know what? No, don't bother answering. Because you don't know anything about the hell you stepped into today. You could have been caught and death would have been kinder than what would have happened. You are NEVER allowed to step foot out of this ship unless I say so. Do you understand me?"

When she didn't answer, it pissed him off more. He didn't know he could get so upset. With fighting speed, he slammed his fist against the scanner, feeling vindicated when it cracked. "Answer me," he said between his teeth.

"You really want my answer?" she asked calmly with a serious edge. "Because you're not going to like it."

"There is only one answer, and you will give it to me."

"So you don't want an answer, you want my obedience?"

"Don't you dare twist this around. I am doing this to keep you safe," he said, closing the distance between them and using his size to force her to comply.

"I know you think so, and I appreciate how much you care. I know that you're drowning in your fears of what could have happened and are getting violent." Her voice was not soothing the wildness inside him.

"I also know that your fears are very real because you lived that hell, in that place, with that awful Demon who did what he did to this male to you. So, I understand you, your rage, your fears, and your desire to control me so you don't lose me. But you aren't going to lose me. Because I'm not fragile. I may not be a Cerebral in name or title, but my abilities helped save someone today. And not in a medical way. In a real rescue kind of way. I have never felt so much...value in my abilities. In my life."

Gammon didn't care to listen to what she said. Nothing would change his mind.

"So, we obviously have a problem. A big one. But right now,

I'm busy. Apparently, I have hundreds of survivors that I need to attend to."

Gammon did not like that either. "And, like I said, rotating them in fives will take a long time."

"Yes, it will. Each patient will need a full scan and most likely medical attention. Considering that you've never been a doctor, I understand how frustrating the medical process is. But there is a process, and I will follow it, especially if it will be uploaded into the Federation archives."

"I don't have to be a doctor to know that it would be faster if —" he started. Suddenly, his mouth and body were frozen.

Amaree lifted two fingers on her right hand and lifted him into the air. "It's one thing to get upset and crazy over my safety. It is another if you think I will allow you to tell me how to do my job. For *your* safety, I suggest you take a walk. A very long one."

Gammon's anger chilled when she floated him out of the medical bay and into the elevator. When he was free, he reached over to open the doors, ready to go talk to her again, but he was re-frozen and forced to hit the button for the bridge.

Once there, she lifted him and brought him in. Kava didn't bother looking at Gammon as he floated past and was set down in the communication's seat.

Standing up, Gammon warned, "Don't get in between my mate and me."

Kava waved at the door. "By all means, go back down there and threaten her some more. I'm sure if you come down on her long enough, she will break, and you'll have a perfect pet-mate."

Fury like Gammon had never known before erupted as he ran at the bastard, who would dare to call Amaree a pet. Kava was on his feet, fists up to block Gammon's first punch. Then like he had been trained, he hit fast and swift, and did everything he could to take down his opponent. To punish Kava for putting Amaree in danger.

Kava was heavy-handed and swift, Gammon got in several hits. Kava got a few of his own in, and by the time Gammon's chest burned from lack of breath, he realized that the Cerebral hadn't used his abilities.

Confused, Gammon staggered back and rested his back against the wall. "I didn't think you could fight fair."

Kava slouched in his chair, his chest rising high from a deep breath. "You make it sound like you won. You didn't."

"I got you a few times, though."

Kava glanced over. "And that makes you special?"

"I feel special," Gammon said with a chuckle, feeling calmer and more emotionally stable.

"Well, I'm not the one bleeding, so I am pretty sure that means I win."

Ass.

Kava chuckled and pointed to a chair. "Why don't you take a seat, Mung can go get us some drinks."

Mung, the blue Semp, held up a hand and pointed to the pilot seat. "Can't. I'm flying the ship."

"It's on autopilot, and you can teleport."

"With you two bruisers, we'll end up crashing into some random planet," he huffed.

"Mung," Kava said, and the Semp teleported. Less than a minute later, Mung returned, tossing them each a Niffy.

"Thanks," Gammon said and upended the bottle, drinking the whole thing. When he finished, he nodded to Kava and headed to the exit.

Kava grunted. "You're a stubborn ass."

"This stubborn ass is going to apologize to his mate before she reconsiders using those nanites."

SEVENTEEN
THE PROLIFIC KING

Amaree stared at the Minky screen, seeing nothing but the look on Gammon's face when she floated him into the elevator. She'd hated doing that, but she was honest to Seth upset. As a doctor, she had seen so many people lose it on their loved ones who just happened to be in the wrong place at the wrong time.

Those people reacted to their fears, which in turn made them unmanageably angry.

She'd had many experiences dealing with people like that, and had used the same calm-yet-assertive voice on her mate. But the difference was, she had to see her mate again, and she was not okay with how quickly he'd turned to wanting to control how she did her job.

Peering down at the Yunkin who had witnessed the whole thing, she noticed that he no longer struggled in his restraints and no longer looked at her with a need for vengeance.

Shrugging, she said, "I'm sorry you had to hear that. That was unprofessional."

The male didn't react to any of her words.

Figuring he didn't want to hear her thoughts, she looked down at his restraints. "I'm going to unlock you, okay? But if you attack me, I will hold you up in the air like the other guy, all right?"

Unlocking the broken-minded male was probably a bad idea, but she had to get him off the bed to switch him with another Yunkin who currently waited outside the door. With a flick of her fingers, all four restraints popped open, and she braced.

Slowly, the Yunkin sat up and slipped off the side of the bed, giving her his back for a second before turning towards her as if making sure she didn't attack him. She looked to the door and said, "Antonis will take you to your room."

The Yunkin walked to the nearest wall and sat down with one knee up, and one leg straight. He assumed a relaxed position, but she wasn't fooled.

Using her ability, she opened the medical door and peered over, seeing Antonis. "Can you bring the next one in?"

Antonis ushered in the male by his chain and cuffed him. When her patient was secure, Amaree said, "Thank you. Can you take the first Yunkin to his room?"

"No."

"Really?" she asked, wondering if he was messing with her.

Antonis walked back towards the door, and she realized that he wasn't joking. "Why not?"

At the door, he said, "Because he is not chained, and he has one of your scalpels."

Amaree looked over at the first Yunkin with a frown. "Are we going to have a problem?"

He moved his eyes to the other Yunkin and didn't look back at her.

"Okay," she said, pulling the cracked scanner over to the bed. "But if you attack me, I will have to take you to a room."

The second Yunkin's treatment went faster, and now that she knew what to look for, she was able to copy a lot of her notes from the first Yunkin's internal damage. When she was done, she told him the same thing. "I'm going to release you. I'd appreciate it if you didn't try to attack me."

Releasing the cuffs with a pop, the second Yunkin quickly jumped from the bed and moved to where the first Yunkin sat. The second Yunkin stood as if he were looking for something from the first, but the first Yunkin simply looked at her, ignoring the second male.

The second male walked on until he stopped at the fourth medbed. He leapt on top of the canopy and a slight groan issued from the device.

The first Yunkin turned and hissed at the second male. The second slid off the bed and sat near the wall.

Amaree opened the medical bay doors and called for the next one. Antonis brought in the third Yunkin and locked him in. "Eventually, the Yunkins will need to be taken to their own rooms," she told him.

"No, they won't."

Holding out her arms, she asked, "What?"

Antonis didn't answer, but he didn't seem happy about something.

Looking down at number three, she heard the first Yunkin hiss again. Apparently, the second male had jumped back up onto the medbed.

Ignoring that, she began her scan, adding the male's medical scans and health procedures to the mission notes. A few minutes later, the first Yunkin hissed again, and she stopped to groan. "Let him sit on the canopy. It won't break."

When she was done with the third ex-slave, she told him the same thing she told the first two. But this one didn't leave the bed when he was free. He also didn't look at her the entire time. The third one seemed to be the most distant.

The first Yunkin got up, yanked the third off the bed, and

dragged him to a spot near the wall. Once the third one was down, the first Yunkin returned to his spot and looked at her again as if waiting for a command—or maybe he expected a compliment for his good work.

She smiled. "You're a strict leader. You remind me of a motis."

His lips pressed together, but he didn't say anything.

"Motis means king. You take charge like a king."

His stiff look eased.

"I think I'm going to call you Motis...at least until you tell me your birth name."

The Yunkin didn't say a word, but she saw his chest puff a little. Pleased to have a name for him, she decided to look at the second Yunkin. "May I call you Nebo?" The Yunkin rubbed his nose with his shoulder but didn't do anything else. Wondering if he might respond if she told him what it meant—not that it meant anything, she had just made it up—she said, "Nebo is the name of the high mountains. They're dangerous and unforgiving to strangers, but the people in the village who live at the base are grateful for their protection and provisions."

Nebo lifted his chin and sniffed. His chest flared a bit, and she was sure that she'd picked the right name.

To the third Yunkin, she was pleased to see that he was looking at her. It wasn't the same way Motis did, but it was less lethal. "You remind me of someone who could care less about everyone and everything. But you're strong, and you'll always find your feet in a fight. If it's okay with you, I'd like to call you Deem."

He didn't seem upset by the name, so she just left it at that. Looking down at the fourth Yunkin, she said, "I don't know enough about you to give you a name. But after this medical check, I'll have one for you, too."

She was halfway through the scans and notes when the

medical door opened, and she smelled her mate. Not sure if he was still in a mood, she didn't turn to him.

Motis, however, stood and moved closer to the medbed she was working from. Nebo slid off the canopy but didn't move any closer, but she could feel the tension rising.

Not trusting the males, she peered over and saw Gammon walking in with a confident gait, but his eyes zeroed in on Motis.

"Hey," she called, hoping to draw his attention. "You calmed down?"

Gammon peered at her for a second and then moved his gaze back to Motis. "Did they get loose?"

"After their medical check, I let them go," she said, knowing he wouldn't like that.

As predicted, he stepped up to her. "Okay. I realize that you have a soft heart, and I absolutely love that about you. But these guard dogs are not safe."

"They're not dogs!" she snapped. "They are Yunkins, and they will be treated with respect."

Gammon's jaw flexed, but he didn't contradict her. "Okay, I will do that...unless one attacks you or anyone else on the crew."

He didn't have to explain what he would do. She got the unspoken threat. And it was a reasonable negotiation. But she didn't want to tell Motis the rules in the format of a threat. "Motis, would you please keep your men from killing the crew? My cousin is the captain. He has yellow eyes, and his mate was the brown-haired one who was with me when we first met. The pilot has blue skin and a tail, then there's the winged guy you've already scared, a Boore, the Boore's mate...I don't exactly know what she looks like, but she's the ship's cook, and they have a daughter...I think that's all of them. No, wait. Prussia. The one with the blue-green and grey skin, and her hair shaved on both sides. And, lastly, the black Kingling. He's not exactly crew, but he's important."

Motis, who had been staring at Gammon, peered over at her and gave a very slight nod. She instantly grinned.

He responded!

A small step, but a big one too because now she was absolutely sure he could understand her. Which was good because she needed to regain control of her workspace.

"Can you two please step back so I can finish my medical check?" Neither male moved, and she had no idea if that was because they were ignoring her or if they were waiting for the other male to move first.

Looking down at the male on the bed, she whispered loud enough for everyone. "We're going to pretend they're not there, okay? If you need to close your eyes to do that, I'll understand."

The male did not close his eyes, but he did make a confused face before tilting his head at her. She talked him through everything she saw on his scans, everything the medbed would heal, and then everything she was marking on his medical file. She made sure to mention what was similar with the other males and what was unique, that way the others were also told about their files.

When she was done, she unlocked the cuffs and pointed at the chiller on the other side of the room. "Thank you for being patient. There are six Niffy drinks in the chiller if you want one."

Nebo was the first to leave his spot for the chiller. The fourth Yunkin hissed as he jumped off the bed and hurdled two medbeds to get to the Niffys. When he arrived, he hit Nebo in the arm and stomach, making the drink fall. The fourth Yunkin caught the drink in the air with one hand while grabbing the other bottles.

"How civilized," Gammon mumbled.

Scoffing, she held out her palm and said, "Ah, did you see

that catch? He simultaneously caught the bottle while grabbing the others."

She waited until the fourth Yunkin looked at her—which he didn't until he finished the first Niffy and ejected the bottle, which was damn civilized. "My cousin Mallik loves Terran sports, specifically baseball. He told me about a family of catchers once that goes back thousands of years. He said that, at any given time, there is always a male from that family who plays. So, I want to call you Molina, but...you also seem to eat and drink like you're ravenous, so maybe Rav is a better name for you."

Rav peered at her, but she didn't think he was actually looking, more like making sure she wouldn't take his drinks.

Amaree called in the last two Yunkins and had them put in two beds on the other side of the room. Antonis told her, "I will begin bringing the fighters in from the brig. But they need to keep their collars on so I can return them."

She didn't think a collar was necessary, and she planned to prove it. But first, she had to finish with her patients. Following the same procedure as before, she explained everything she was doing and then let them up and gave them a name.

All six had moved to various areas around the medical bay. She knew that she had a lot of checks to go through, so she asked the six and Gammon if they were hungry. Gammon nodded, and she quickly called the cook, pleased to speak to the Boore's mate for the first time. Happily, she learned that her name was Pasha, and asked if she could send down some food, Niffys and desserts if she had any.

Pasha arrived before Antonis. Rav tried taking all the food, so she had to float him with a plate, but gave him control of himself so he could eat. The rest were able to take a plate and eat in their respective corners.

Of course, Gammon and Motis ate near her, and she was

able to take a few bites before Antonis came in with the first fighter. He looked vicious. The male was pulling, kicking, slicing, and biting at the winged male.

As one...all the males in the medical bay stood. The six hissed low in their throats, and Gammon growled.

The fighter jerked around and, no joke, when he saw Motis, the color in his face drained. Gammon looked back at Motis, and by the love of Seth, the Yunkin looked as if he were a true king of death.

Amaree could practically smell his arrogance.

Gammon peeked at her, and they shared a moment. In that second, she felt all the anger and hurt settle. This was her mate. And, yes, they would have issues as they went through different stressful situations, but there was an undeniable connection, and she loved him.

She didn't care that it would make no sense to her parents or her cousins or anyone else. She loved her mate, and she was sure that no matter what happened between them, they could work it out. Because they had an undeniable bond.

Antonis got the male near the medbed. Motis helped to strap him down because right before he was put in the bed, the fighter tried to get free.

Gammon didn't watch the situation as he blocked her view. His hand moved to touch her face but he held back, and she hated seeing the look of doubt on his face. "I'm sorry. I'm sorry I yelled at you and broke your medical stuff, then said you couldn't do anything without my permission."

She appreciated his softly spoken words because they weren't for everyone, but now wasn't the time. She tried to say his name but paused when Antonis walked past.

"Gammon," she started as he grabbed the back of her neck and brought her to him so their foreheads touched.

"Don't take the nanites," he said in a voice that was barely breathed, let alone said.

Her heart squeezed at the realization that he thought she would do that. Even though it was the worst time to address this very personal issue, she touched his chest and trilled at him.

He trilled back, and his grip on her neck increased for a second. She could only imagine how much he was holding back. When he let go, he cleared his throat. He stepped back, giving her room but not leaving the area.

She didn't look at Motis because this was the second time he'd had to witness their mating issues.

Hours later, she took a break between medical checks. She had Gammon bring some snacks for everyone and, again, she had to hold up Rav, who seemed to like that he was up high—as if no one could touch his food up there.

Gammon and her had another moment as if he too noticed Rav's peculiar relaxed state of eating. Unlike last time, she sat with him as they ate. She even kissed him on the shoulder. "Thanks for getting the food."

"Not worth mentioning. It wasn't hard to carry."

"No, but you had to leave me with six males."

He shrugged as if that too weren't worth mentioning.

In her head, Kava's voice surprised her, and she sat straight up. "*Admiral Rannn is asking for you two. I have him on the Minky screen on the bridge.*"

Gammon held out his hand for her plate and was about to set them aside when he gave them back and pointed at Rav. She floated them up and then closed out the file she hadn't yet processed and closed. Once she did that, she brought Rav down. All the food was gone, and she chuckled.

To Motis, she said, "Admiral Rannn is on a call upstairs. He's asking for us so we'll be right back."

Motis looked at Deem and Nebo, and they jumped to their feet and moved to his flanks. When she and Gammon walked out, she realized that all three followed, leaving Immit and Zane in the medical bay. "What are you doing?"

No one answered.

She looked at Gammon for answers. He shrugged as if he didn't know, but the smell of his amusement gave him away.

"Uh, okay, just remember no hurting anyone, all right?"

Again, they didn't say anything, but she didn't expect them to. They followed her and Gammon into the elevator and then onto the bridge. She could see the back of Kava's head, where he sat in the captain's chair. Fenton sat on the left arm of the seat as the blue Semp piloted the ship. Rannn's pale face and hair were on screen, and he didn't sound happy as he spoke. "We are not getting involved in a battle between the king and the Kinglings on Port Nicca. Need I remind you that we are trying to form an alliance *not* start a war?"

"The fight may be between the Kinglings, but I can promise you that all the other people will suffer for it. And if we don't get down there and help, the wrong one may end up winning," Fenton snapped.

"Who's the wrong one?" Rannn asked with an unsettling threat.

"The king," Fenton said as she got off the armrest. Kava's face was turned toward her, and it looked as if they were facing off in a silent battle.

"Officer Fenton, you apparently forgot the whole point of this mission: to form an alliance with the king so the Federation and our citizens can begin expanding into the unused worlds without resistance. Having the king as an ally will go far in the Outworlds."

"Yeah, I know, but you're wrong. The king is a ruthless bastard. He only uses his influence when threatening someone who offends him. He has no ties, and he will never vouch for the Federation," Fenton said, both fists clenched at her sides.

"King Azze puts more value on his bloodline than anything else," Rannn seethed. "So, this is the best chance we have."

Fenton spoke through her teeth. "You don't know him."

"And you do?" Rannn challenged.

"I was raised on Nicca. I've heard the stories from his ex-warriors."

Entering into the background of the call, Gammon said, "Ex-warriors would be biased against a king who found them lacking."

Fenton cut her eyes at him, and for a moment, Amaree was almost scared for him.

"People who feel the most wronged have the loudest voices," Gammon added firmly.

Amaree didn't know the king of the Kinglings, but she could feel the passion in which Fenton spoke, and she worried that maybe her mate was wrong. But she also agreed with what Gammon had said about those who felt wronged speaking up the most.

"Coming out of quantum drive. We are closing in on Port Nicca now Captain," said the Semp from the pilot's seat.

Rannn spoke to Gammon. "Get the alliance and complete the mission." To her, he said, "I've seen the updates in the mission notes. When this is over, transfer all of the survivors to Pegna. I will have Arvey see if he can do anything to help them. If not, then they will be transported to the Terran planet for extensive therapy."

Absolutely. He could have all the fighters in the brig. "Yes, sir," Amaree agreed.

"Good," Rannn said but then looked behind her and

frowned. "Who are those three behind you?"

"Motis, Deem, and Nebo."

"Are they from Pawwai?"

"No," she said, knowing they hadn't been born there. "They are helping me with scanning and attending to all the survivors."

Rannn nodded, but she wasn't sure if he believed her. His last words were to Gammon, repeating his objective. It wasn't until Rannn terminated the call that Fenton stabbed a finger at Kava and hissed, "Don't."

Mung, the Semp, yelled, "Incoming torpedoes."

"Who the hell is firing at us?" Kava asked, sitting forward.

"Does it matter? Are we planning on sending them a gift basket?" Mung yelled back as he jerked the controls to the right.

"I hate Cerebral blockers," Kava said as he moved to the visual navigation screen.

Fenton turned on her heel and headed for the door. Gammon moved to the weapons and tactical seat and powered up the screen. He moved with so much confidence that she knew he was in his element.

Turning to the exit, she told the Yunkins, "I'm going to make sure she's okay. I'll be right back."

As nimbly as she could, Amaree exited the bridge and saw the elevator doors closing. The footsteps behind her told her that the Yunkins had followed, so she melted the floor and fell through.

The elevator had not opened, so Amaree went to the next level and then the next...all the way to the cargo bay. Fenton rushed out, saw her, and said, "You're not stopping me."

"Nope," Amaree said as she caught up to Fenton.

Pointing at the lifepods, Fenton said, "Come on, before the stupid Federation sides with that bastard, Azze."

As insane as it was, Amaree smiled as she ran next to

Fenton. The buzz of adrenaline began pumping in her veins.

"Our first objective, of course, is to not get killed. Do you have a medscope?"

"I have one in my pocket," Amaree said, shoving her hand into her pocket and wishing she had her frostic knife.

When they got to the pods, Fenton got in a two-seater and pulled out a Minky pad. Amaree followed. The doors shut, and before she could strap in, the weightlessness of discharging from the Maw wiggled her stomach. Sitting down, Amaree strapped in and asked, "So, what exactly are we going to do to save the Outworlds?"

Tapping on the Minky screen with a dexterity that Amaree would never possess, the female whispered a series of words to herself that made no sense to Amaree. When she stopped, the pod began vibrating, letting both of them know that they were entering the planet's atmosphere.

"Anytime you want to tell me the plan, that would be great," Amaree said, holding on tightly, knowing the pod's thrusters would kick in any second.

The pod landed with a thud, and Fenton stood, stuffing the Minky pad into her pocket as she hit the door's ejection button. "Basically, we have to stop Nicca from being annihilated."

"What?" Amaree said, following Fenton out of the pod and into a vast desert.

Fenton clapped her hands twice and pointed to where an explosion had happened. "We need to go that way, and we need to go fast. Every inch of the planet outside the city is full of things that want to eat us. We need to get in the air."

Amaree took the lifepod door and made them a flat surface to sit on as they moved. She liked it better. She could see if anyone was going to attack. Fenton pointed to a puff of fine dust that burst up from the air on her right. "That is a giant sand barbist. You need to stay away from it."

A giant sand barbist? Barbists were already massive-sized snakes with a mouth full of teeth instead of just two fangs.

Another puff of dust shot into the air, this time on their left.

Fenton cursed. "We're in its mouth."

"In its *mouth*?" Amaree asked while taking in the distance between both puffs of dust. If that was true, the beast was...

The dry lakebed shot up into the air like a wall of sand, and Amaree saw the many hundreds of sharp, pointed teeth. Her heart stopped as the sunlight practically disappeared and they were swallowed up.

Focusing her mind, she brought Fenton back under her and then remolded the metal flying door to a sharp point to act like a bullet. She gritted her teeth, hoping the barbist's skin wasn't impenetrable.

The pointed end cut through the skin, coating them in barbist ichor, and the massive thing let out a pained cry.

Without looking back, Amaree remolded the door and set Fenton and her back down. Fenton looked back and scoffed. "You blew a hole in its throat." With a nod of approval, she said, "You fool a pirate queen to kidnap her prisoner, rip whole ships apart, save savages, and kill mega-snakes with an impromptu bullet. Songs should be written about you."

Amaree shook her head at the insanity of it all, but in the same breath, it was all true, and she felt good about that.

To her left, a small sloop changed directions and came straight at her. The ship fired two torpedoes, and Amaree didn't have to put much effort into turning them around and making them fly back at the ship that'd fired them.

"The pirate witch strikes again," Fenton said before facing forward.

Amaree snorted but kept an eye on the battle. Raising the door, she wanted to get altitude to better observe the fight. With a high-point view, she saw the thousands of sloops dotting the left side of the city. Six galleon ships sat on the landing pads, and one of them was burning. Each one had the symbol of a gold lightning bolt on the hull.

Amaree knew that symbol. It was the pirate queen's.

To the left, a horde of people ran through the many tents, ripping them apart along with everyone inside. From where Amaree flew, she could see that some were Kinglings, and the rest were pirates.

Heading straight into the melee, both she and Fenton ran in opposite directions. Amaree went after the Kingling dressed in silver armor with a black crest of thorns. Part of her wished to kill him straightaway, but instead, she flicked her fingers and melted the armor to surround him like a cocoon.

She did the same to the Kingling ransacking the tent, and the one about to slice his sword through a pair of elderly females huddled together. When the Kingling was neutralized, the two women picked up his sword and used it to stab where his head was.

Amaree ran to the next tent and saw another Kingling not dressed in the same armor, but that didn't change the fact that he attacked her. So, she melted his weapon.

The dark purple Kingling stared at his empty hands. "This can't be a dream. I'm sure it's not."

Just then, another Kingling in armor came at the blue one and sliced at him. The Kingling turned and used his large, reptilian tail to knock over the attacker. Seeing that he was attacking the same people, she flicked her hand and gave him back his sword.

The Kingling understood then, saying, "Thanks," before slicing the air and gutting the attacker.

Amaree ran through the streets, checking the tents that were still upright to make sure they were all empty. After five empty shelters, she heard a double boom—the sound of a massive ship entering the atmosphere.

Peering up, Amaree saw what looked like a black dot. But it wasn't black, it was red.

Kava.

More confident, Amaree moved away from the empty tents and ran towards the landing docks.

"Hey. Where are you going?" Fenton called as Amaree ran past.

Amaree pointed to the docks as if the answer should have been common knowledge. Her mate was on the Maw. Her crew. Help.

"No, we need to find out why the king is attacking," Fenton said and then pointed out a male with a gold lightning bolt tattoo on his face that rounded the corner with a phaser.

Amaree quickly froze the male to keep him from hurting them.

"Perfect, let's ask him," Fenton said, and Amaree brought the male forward. Fenton took the phaser from his hands and pointed it between his legs. "If you don't want to die bleeding to death from the loss of this *limb*, tell me why the king's warriors and the pirate queen's minions are attacking."

"Vengeance," he said from between his blackened teeth.

"Given the level of violence, that's obvious," Amaree said as she squeezed his body a bit. "What my friend wants to know is why they're seeking vengeance."

"Because the king's son was kidnapped by that bastard Moddoe and sold to the Exoworlds where we found him. We're here to level the port and kill the betrayer."

Amaree looked at Fenton, who frowned. "The queen found the king's son in the Exoworlds?"

"On Gabbet."

"What's the son's name?" Fenton asked as she lowered the

phaser.

"Simmer."

Fenton nodded at Amaree as if she were done with him, so Amaree let him go. The second the pirate was on his feet, he swung to punch Fenton in the face, but Amaree flicked her fingers and broke his femur.

The pirate went down with a wail.

Fenton turned and spoke as if the male's cries didn't bother her at all. "When I looked at the records for the Kingling planet, it didn't say the king lost two sons. The one I tracked should have been on Gabbet, but I didn't know his name. When I called in Antonis to get a map of the Exoworlds, Gammon told Antonis that the son's name was Oxus, and Antonis pointed us away from the Exoworlds to Pawwai. Which means, Oxus was likely one of the many sons who mysteriously got sick and died. And if the king is *here,* then he's already been reunited with Simmer and has a planet of warriors to call on until the whole port is dust. It's Kingling law to seek out vengeance against a betrayer."

Amaree wasn't sure if Fenton was looking for advice, but she gave it anyway. "Does the king have jurisdiction on this planet?"

"Kind of. I think the Kinglings pay taxes to him."

"Are any of the laws different between the king's planet and here?"

Fenton's eyes lit up. "Yes. Here, you don't have to be a Kingling to seek vengeance for an offense. As long as you're a citizen, you can challenge your offender."

"We need to find a citizen," Amaree said, glancing around.

"I'm a citizen. I grew up here. It's my home planet. I will always be a citizen," Fenton said happily.

"Great, now what offense can you accuse the king of?"

Fenton looked away. Her eyes turned glossy, and Amaree

knew she wasn't paying attention, which was why Amaree broke both arms of the pirate who rounded the corner.

With no warning, Fenton turned and pointed to the burning part of the city. "Kava says the king's this way."

Amaree ran beside her and flung all the attackers out of their way. Once they reached the heat of the burning buildings, she saw a handful of young Kinglings watching the fire with swords in their hands.

"Fire bad," she said, realizing too late that she'd forgotten a word or two.

Fenton led the way around the side of the building and cut through a pass at the back that wove between mud walls and burning cloths used to cover the roofs.

Then, right before they ducked under the last post, something pushed them back and held them against the mud walls.

Amaree felt the presence of her cousin, but no words entered her mind.

"Kava says that you need to wait for your bodyguards and mate," Fenton said quickly.

"You can't go in there by yourself. I don't even need to see what's past that wall to know it's dangerous," Amaree said, knowing Kava could hear her.

"Kava will take me over and get me to the king."

"That's one way to do it," Amaree said, wondering why Kava wasn't just joining them, but then she remembered that only citizens could challenge the king, and Kava wasn't.

"Okay, I'm going in."

"Wait, are we sure this is going to work?"

"Absolutely. Kinglings respect lethal warriors. With Kava making me look like a god, King Azze will acknowledge my challenge."

Good to know, Amaree thought before Fenton slipped under the archway and disappeared into the noise of the melee.

EIGHTEEN
SOMEHOW, IT'S ALWAYS PIRATES

The ship came to a stop, and Gammon hit the button to open the ramp, surrounded by the six guard dogs and fifty-six Demon fighting slaves.

"This is where we get off, right?" Qraw asked.

"That's the plan!" Gammon said as the descending ramp was barely low enough to see the battle. It had not fully extended, but the six strays his mate had brought home and fed jumped off the ledge as one in a perfectly executed leap. They hit the ground with a roll and ended in a full-out run.

"I feel sorry for whoever they're after," Qraw said, shaking his head.

Gammon didn't. He had seen how they'd looked at Amaree. Not one smelled of lust or hatred. Motis was the one who stood closest to her, and all Gammon could smell was possessiveness.

Jumping from the ship so as not to be outdone by his mate's guards, Gammon hit the ground harder than expected but got up and started running. Taking a deep breath, he searched for his mate's scent. It took almost five minutes for him to catch it, but then it was on.

Motis and the others diverted from their current path to follow him.

Her scent led him to the burning building and then behind it. Worried that she might have been taken by someone, he pushed his legs harder as he followed an insane crisscross of walls and mud archways with burning roofs of straw, sticks, and cloth.

He was relieved to find Amaree alone in a small alcove. He figured she'd come back here to hide from the battle. But the happy look in her eyes when she saw him turned serious, and she pointed at the archway. "Fenton has a plan. We need to go and help," she said and entered through an archway. He and the six followed.

As they entered an open field that wasn't visible from the other side of the building, the six quickly surrounded Amaree and attacked everyone within reach. The massive mob of fighters outnumbered any modern battle he had participated in while a W&T commander.

In the distance, he saw a warship with a black thorn crest on its nose. It was bigger than a galleon, and Federation galleon's held thousands of people. Considering the other Kingling ships that had attacked them in space, this one had to be the king's.

Amaree and her six Yunkins moved through the crowd like a worm removing everything in its path. As he followed, he saw that all of the king's warriors were being cocooned in their own armor and falling like dud torpedoes.

Gammon knew his mate and that the males inside were alive. In his heart, he was grateful that Fenock of Fortune gave him a softhearted, stubborn, and courageous mate.

As he followed, two pirates with phasers turned to him after shooting a Kingling not dressed in silver armor. Gammon avoided the first shot because the shooters had been bumped from behind, but the second shooter got him in the upper chest.

The smell of ozone was thick in the air, and Gammon knew it was more than Amaree's simple melting of the armor.

Covering the wound with his hand, he looked around for Amaree, worried that Kava would break the planet. Reaching out to grab the nearest pirate and rip out his throat, Gammon paused because of their limp facial expressions.

A red line appeared on their throats, and then their heads slowly toppled back and bounced as they hit the dirt.

Gammon watched in horror as more heads fell to the ground. A mixture of pirates and the king's warriors. The bodies followed, and Gammon noticed Qraw and the other Demons from Pawwai standing like sentinels, perfectly spaced, their faces devoid of emotion.

What the hell were they doing here?

Less than a hundred Kinglings were left standing, and none were the king's warriors. Amaree and her six Yunkins stood behind Fenton, who waited directly in front of the pure black-scaled Kingling dressed in silver armor.

He held his two-handed sword with its electric blue current loosely at his side, the edges glowing. A small ways off was the glowing pirate queen.

Next to the queen stood a black-and-grey-scaled Kingling, dressed in worn pants with several holes. That Kingling looked at the dead bodies with terrifying confusion.

"What witchcraft is this?" the black Kingling hissed.

"You attacked my home, King Azze," Fenton shouted.

"Who the hell are you?" the king snarled.

Gammon moved between two of the Yunkins and stood next to his mate. He was close enough to discern the King's fear and rage.

Ignoring the king, Fenton asked, "Why did you attack my home?"

The king snarled again, and Gammon smelled deception

before the male even opened his mouth. "You're a powerful witch, you should already know. Or maybe you waited until now to kill my warriors to try and intimidate me. You knew I was coming. You knew I found out about Moddoe's betrayal. And you set a trap."

"If I knew you were coming, I would have stopped you before you entered the atmosphere."

The king chuckled arrogantly, but Gammon was still stuck on what Fenton had said. She acted like she lived on the planet. Not only that, but it almost sounded as if she was taking responsibility for Kava's beheading.

"It's easy to be bold when speaking of things you haven't done," the king condemned.

"Is it just as bold to decide the fate of a warrior without speaking to him first...or even getting evidence?" Fenton challenged, and Gammon was displeased at the smell of wrath.

The king gripped his sword tighter, making it easier to swing and slice Fenton in half. Hatred dripped from every word as the king explained, "Moddoe was there when my son disappeared. I trusted him. He had never failed me before. Not until he failed to find my boy."

"And his failure to find your son somehow equaled his guilt?"

"Who are you to challenge my judgment? As king, it is my right to rule as I choose."

There was a silent, uncomfortable pause before Fenton nodded. "Yes, it is."

King Azze snorted from his large, reptilian nostrils. "Your agreement sounds insincere."

"I'm not disagreeing that you have a right to lead your people as you wish," Fenton began. "But you're not the king of this planet. Here, the law dictates that you're accountable for your actions."

The yellow eyes in the deep-set black reptilian face narrowed. "You dare judge me?"

"I do dare," Fenton said. "And everyone here will be my witnesses." With a dramatic flair, she turned halfway and gestured to the surviving Kinglings of Port Nicca.

The king snarled as he grabbed the hilt with his other hand and got halfway into his swing before something flung him back as if he were a bug being flicked by an invisible giant. He landed hard with his sword at his side.

The ozone in the air was thick once more, and Gammon knew it wasn't Amaree because he was standing right next to her. Ozone filled the air, and he assumed it was Kava but asked Amaree to make sure. "How is she doing that?" he breathed.

"Kava," Amaree whispered back.

Right.

Like he'd thought.

It took Azze several moments before he sat up and stared at Fenton from a distance. Eyes tense, Gammon saw the moment King Azze realized that he was no match for his opponent. Then just as abruptly, the king floated off the ground and returned to his original spot, his weapon left in the dirt.

Fenton began by pointing to her left. The yellow Kingling, Moddoe, floated in the air towards them. The blue shoulder sash he usually wore was gone, but the large brown-and-black beaded necklace was still wrapped around his neck. His chest was bare and bleeding from several wounds, but for a Kingling, that wouldn't have slowed him down.

As soon as his feet hit the ground, he eyed the king with disdain. When his eyes fell on Fenton, he smiled. "Fenton? I wondered why I saw you racing across the desert."

"My home was being attacked," she said.

Moddoe's distrust turned to cunning pleasure. "That it was, wasn't it?"

Gammon could literally smell the conspiracy between the two.

Fenton turned back to the king. "I stand against you, King Azze, as your accuser. As a citizen of Port Nicca, I challenge you to a battle of arms until death—or until you surrender."

The king held out his arms. "I accept this fight so long as you don't use your witch spells."

"I can't stop being what I am," she replied. "But I don't want you to surrender, so I won't use telekinesis against you."

Azze grinned. "Just so you know, when I win, I'm going to kill Moddoe and then order all of my warriors from the whole planet to come here and decimate every living person left alive, including your family and friends."

Fenton held up her fists and moved her weight between her toes. It was a good stance, but against a Kingling, Gammon couldn't imagine Fenton fighting without Kava's help.

Azze threw a one-two punch that Fenton dodged, but he tripped her with his large tail when he whirled around. Landing with a grunt, Fenton looked stunned. Gammon's stomach lurched as Azze noticed, too.

With a slap of his tail, crushing down on her chest, Fenton moaned, and her eyes closed.

Azze sneered as he loomed over her and said, "To the death, then." Reaching back, he wound up to crush her face when she unclipped a small blue cloth bag from her belt and threw it at his face.

Jerking back, the king shook his head. Then he began to sneeze, one after another until he stumbled backwards. In between sneezes, he accused, "Witchcraft."

Fenton snickered. "No, you ass. It's called research. You had an allergic reaction to mellow-vine when you first became king. Your warriors were then sent to cut down and burn every mellow-vine bush on the planet."

Shaking his head, the king sneezed again and again, unable to stop. Fenton walked over and held up a glass vial. "Surrender, and I'll give you the antihistamine medicine."

"Give...it to...me," he hissed.

"You have to say the words."

"GIVE...it to...me. I surrender!"

Fenton handed over the vial, and he gulped the contents in one go. Within seconds, he was breathing better but still hunched over. "I've never surrendered in my life."

"I read that, too," Fenton said. "While you're down there, I have a story to tell you. About thirty or so years ago, the Federation started making plans to lay down roots in the Outworlds. They sent several of their top commanders to find out how to do that. The commanders came back with a unanimous vote that if they got an alliance with you, they'd have access to all the Outworlds."

Azze snorted. "I don't make alliances."

"Oh, I know that, but the idiots running the Federation don't."

Gammon felt slapped. Apparently, he was wrong about the king. Very wrong.

"Less than a week ago," she continued, "the Federation hired me to find your son and return him to you as a gesture of good faith with hopes of an alliance."

The king looked more interested then.

"The thing was, they hired me because the original mission failed. The male behind me with the dark hair was kidnapped by the pirate queen, who was informed by a betrayer in the Federation that Gammon was on the hunt for what would win the Federation your allegiance. So, of course, the queen kidnapped Gammon and tortured out any and all information he had. Thankfully, he's a dud when it comes to research."

The king then looked at the pirate queen, who had not

moved. Gammon realized it was because a Cerebral had frozen her stiff.

"When I started my search, I read the reports on your son, who was about five when they took him from your home planet. I did hundreds of searches on all the ships on or around your planet at the time. The best leads I found led back to your healer, who had given a delivery rather than picking one up. Which was odd. But I'll get to that later. The delivery took off from your planet and left the Outworlds. Given my estimates, he ended up on Gabbet—a remote planet where people live underground."

Shaking his head, the king looked dumbfounded.

"I appreciate you thinking that I did some kind of magic, but it's not that complicated. I'm a Numan with overwhelming intelligence."

Gammon couldn't fight the smile that pulled at his lips. Fenton was a Numan? She sure didn't act like one...in the medical sense, anyway, but if he thought about it, he could see it.

"Now, by the time I was hired, your son was no longer on the planet. I assumed that someone, most likely the pirate queen, already had him. But then I learned you lost another son."

"I only lost Simmer," the king said, pointing to the black-and-grey-spotted Kingling who crossed his arms, listening to Fenton's story.

"Do you remember Oxus?"

Azze turned away. "Yes. He was a pure color like me. The only one to be blessed by Fenock. He and his mother died from a disease when he was very young."

"Your son Oxus is on my ship."

Azze's eyes snapped to her.

"Remember that odd thing I mentioned about your healer?

Yeah, well, that female has probably been poisoning your sons for years. Because there is no way a disease affects your family line and no one else's. Not to mention, the few that survive are not in your favor, are they?"

Oh, hell. Gammon wiped a hand over his mouth. Azze had hundreds of children, and almost all of them had died. Gammon would lose his mind if he found out that they were being poisoned.

Fenton turned around and held out her hand. Amaree walked over and handed her a medscope. Giving it to the king, she said, "Take this medscope home with you and give it to your sick son, who's been ill for months. It will heal him. And if you don't break it, it will last for years."

The Kingling took it and stood. Soberly, he whispered, "You really have Oxus?"

"I do," she said.

"Take me to him."

"With pleasure. But before I do, you owe me a boon for your surrender. The favor I require is that you and your royal line never attack here ever again. In fact, once you leave, you and your warriors will never step foot on this planet again."

"Agreed," Azze said with a nod.

Fenton turned and headed to the exit. The king trailed. Then Amaree and her six guards followed. He, of course, walked by her side as her guards walked behind. After them, the fifty-six moved in perfect order as they systematically turned on their heels and followed.

NINETEEN
IF IT HAS VALUE, IT CAN BE A TREASURE

Amaree watched with heartbreaking sadness as the king rubbed his head. "Is he sick?"

Being the doctor, Amaree told him, "No. The hundreds of years of abuse at the hands of a Red Demon have left your son this way."

"A medscope won't heal him?" Azze asked, folding his arms over his chest.

"No," Amaree said softly. "His issues are from behavioral conditioning, not broken bones or lacerations. Missing limbs or poison. Those are the things medscopes heal."

Azze held a fist to his mouth. "Where is this Red Demon?"

"Dead," Gammon said from beside Amaree. "And as much as you want to claim the rights to his death, I suffered for hundreds of years at the Demon's feet so I deserved to be the one to take his life."

Azze's nostrils flared. "What planet? I will go and get vengeance on everyone he befriended."

"The planet's been destroyed," Gammon said while squeezing her hand.

"How thorough," Azze said before looking back at his son,

who had not even acknowledged his father's presence. Oxus stayed curled on the floor at the king's feet. "I deserve retribution."

"Take it out on your healer," Fenton suggested.

Azze spoke with sorrow. "The healer will be punished, but she is female, and the things I would love to do to her can't be done. Kinglings do not attack the females of our race—since there are so few."

Silence stretched for a time, and then Amaree found herself asking, "What will happen if you take him back with you?"

The king closed his eyes, and a pained look crossed his reptilian brow ridge. "He can't come with me. His weakness would be challenged, and he would die shortly after arriving. Then, whoever killed my son would challenge me. Even if the warrior didn't win, the doubt would set in, and every successful warrior would challenge me."

Amaree pressed her fingers to her lips, worried that Oxus would spiral worse at the rejection.

"If I was my father, I would kill him here and now to keep the universe from ever knowing about him."

So Azze saw it as a mercy? Amaree again pushed by confirming, "But you're not him, are you?"

Azze's thin lips pulled back in a sad smile. "No. I've lost too many sons." Turning to Fenton, he asked, "I have a boon to ask of you, and I will give whatever you want in return."

"What do you want?" Fenton asked, crossing her arms.

"Keep Oxus. Keep him safe. Let him live out the rest of his life in peace. I will pay you five hundred thousand keleps a year to ensure that you do not have to sacrifice for him."

Amaree felt her heart jump for joy because Oxus wasn't going to leave. She was sure that Oxus would do better with them than with anyone else. He had undergone too much trauma and abuse to snap into the male he was supposed to be—who he could have been.

As he grew as part of the crew, he would have to decide who to be. The fighting slaves would have years of therapy, too, but they were dangerous.

"Oxus will not need your keleps, but I agree to keep him safe," Fenton said as if she were the captain. "As for the boon you offered, I'd like an alliance."

The king leaned back and opened his mouth...then shut it. A long, pregnant pause drew on for minutes. "Until my reign is over, you, Fenton, have my favor. The alliance is between you and me. I will not fight for the Federation or their political games. But if you ever need anything from me, you only have to ask."

"That's all I want. And if you ever need anything, I will fight for you too," she said, and Amaree heard her mate grunt with approval.

Amaree was happy for Gammon. The mission was a success.

The king left without another glance at his son. Prussia came from the far side of the room to whisper something to Oxus, and the male lifted his head. With a little more coaxing, he got up and left with her.

Fenton pointed at Gammon and said, "Bet you didn't think I'd get an alliance, did ya?"

"As if you planned that." He snorted.

"I did," she said with a raised voice but winked at Amaree.

"Right," Gammon said, but it was clear he didn't believe her. He turned, and Amaree followed what he was looking at. Ten Night Demons entered the ship. One jerked his chin in greeting.

"Forget something, Qraw?"

"Food's better on the Maw," said a Night Demon—apparently named Qraw.

"It's not a cafeteria. And the captain said you'd get off at Port Nicca," Gammon shot back.

Qraw tapped his temple. "Cap already agreed we could stay."

"Did he?" Gammon said with the tone he'd used to challenge Fenton.

Motis, who was on Amaree's other side, snapped his head to the exit and hissed under his breath. Amaree followed his gaze and saw Moddoe, the yellow Kingling, walk in as regal as any sovereign with a light blue sash over one shoulder and a darker wrap covering his lower body. He had beads the same color as hers around his neck. The only difference was, his here bigger.

As he entered the cargo bay, his light, charismatic voice carried as he called, "Permission to come aboard?"

"Permission granted, so long as I get free and unlimited access to your inventory," Fenton grinned.

"Absolutely," he said, stopping in front of her. "Just let me know when you plan to stop by so I can be closed and on an important hunt."

"I saved you and the planet, and I don't even get free clothes?" Fenton said with mock offense. "See if I save you again."

Moddoe chuckled and pulled a dagger from the waistband of his blue leather pants. The dagger's sheath looked like white and purple opal. He held it out with one hand.

Fenton's nostrils flared. "You told me you couldn't get another one."

"I didn't."

"This was the one from your shop? The one you said someone bought?" she accused.

"It was bought. By me." Moddoe didn't look at all shy at

what he'd done, and Amaree felt the small tug from Gammon to leave. But Amaree was too nosy to not find out more.

"You rotten-tailed bastard," Fenton snapped. "You knew I wanted it and that I had earned the money to buy it."

He tilted his head like a parent would to a child who was trying to lie to them. "Fen, you spent weeks in your room after I told you the price of the dagger. When you emerged, you headed straight to my gambling cave and cleaned out my dealers *and* my storage safe."

Eyebrows high, Fenton spat back, "I would have gone to another gambling cave, but *you* tripled the price of the dagger."

Shrugging, he said, "It was a special dagger."

"Eat white poop, you toga-Roman-god wannabe."

Amaree had to drop her head because she was literally shaking with laughter. Oddly enough, so was Moddoe. "That was especially colorful."

Fenton reached over and plucked the dagger from his hand then walked off with a mumbled, "Thank you."

"You're welcome, you overwhelmingly intelligent brat," Moddoe called after her.

He swung his long, reptilian face towards her. "Amaree," he cooed. "My prime."

Amaree snorted. "Your...what?"

Moddoe had taken a step towards her, and as one, all six of her Yunkin guards stepped forward with an unnatural hiss. Amazingly, the Kingling clapped. "I knew the moment I saw you as a baby that you'd be a strong and cunning warrior. Barbuck herself whispered it in my ear. And here you are with six pets at your side, and the mating smell of a Rata—the unholy offspring of Fenock's nightmares."

"Excuse me," Amaree said, because that was rude. "My mate is not an unholy offspring."

"It's custom for Kinglings to insult a friend in a complimentary way," Gammon said with a light squeeze of her hand.

Still, he was rude, and she wasn't a Kingling. "These Yunkins are my friends. They aren't pets."

"They have a predator's presence," Moddoe remarked. Before she was able to comment on that, he added, "While leading a group of innocents to the hunting caves, I can't tell you how shocked I was to see a pair of females flying on a thin metal strip and be swallowed up by a sand barbist, only to end up coming out of its throat. Then, seconds later, you turned around two torpedoes."

Amaree worried how Gammon would react to that story. She hoped that if he were upset, he would hold it in until they were alone.

Moddoe grabbed a bracer from his wrist and handed it to her. It was black vanadium. "I spoke to my hunters after you left the battlefield. They told me you trapped the king's warriors in their armor and left them to slowly cook to death. I think that kind of psychological fighting deserves a warrior's gift."

Still not pleased, she took the gift because not taking it might be offensive. "Thank you."

With a polite nod, Moddoe turned to leave when Amaree asked, "What is a prime?"

Pointing to her necklace, he said, "The beads you wear are a symbol that you are a prime of the goddess, Barbuck."

"I can't be a prime to a goddess I don't know."

He shrugged as if he didn't care. "You'll get to know her well enough when I die, and you take over Port Nicca."

"Whaaaaat?" Amaree said, not sure if she believed such a thing.

Moddoe smiled. "Thankfully, you mated a Rata and will share his long life. Not to mention the annoying trait of coming back to life. Unless you cut off their heads. That usually keeps them dead."

Mother of Seth.

The Kingling turned, swishing his tail happily from left to right as he left. The walking reptile had to know he'd just dropped a bomb of insane information about her future and her mate's race.

"Oh, wow," Gammon said, pulling her towards him.

"Yeah, wow. Did you know that you come back to life?" she asked.

"It's as great as it sounds. I've lost count how many times I woke up in a pile of dead bodies. Always figured the people who thought I was dead were idiots."

Oh.

"But more importantly, while doing research in the Outworlds for powerful alliances, I was told that some planets have a god or goddess that rule through their primes. Port Nicca must be one of those."

Amaree had no idea what to say to that. How was that more important than his immortal-like race?

Gammon changed the subject. "Kava just told me that he's calling Admiral Rannn to confirm that the mission is complete. I'm going to join them on the bridge and then I'll meet you in our cabin."

Wincing, she said, "I need to finish the medical checks."

"You will, but we still need to have a talk."

Talk? As in the talk about him getting upset at her and telling her how to do her job? Or was this a chat about leaving the Maw to go to a planet under attack? Or maybe it was about one day taking over a bloody planet?

Actually, she could use some time to think about that one while he was on the bridge. "Okay. I'll be in the cabin."

His eyes warmed, and she smelled his lust. She realized that he might not actually want to *talk*.

An hour and a half later, Gammon walked into their cabin, making a face and pointing at the door with his thumb. Amaree knew he was silently asking about the Yunkins who were sitting outside their room.

Swatting at the air, she didn't want to get into it. She told them they could have any room on the ship they wanted, and neither responded.

Changing topics, she asked, "So, was Rannn happy the mission went well?"

Gammon grabbed her neck and pulled her in for a kiss, heating her from her toes to her head. Assuming that Rannn was happy, she was fine not getting into it. Pressing her hands to his chest, she leaned into the kiss.

He broke the embrace, and she frowned.

Gammon nipped her lip as a chastisement to wait as he unfastened her top. "Rannn said that our plan was reckless and that the council would not be happy about the king's alliance with Fenton, but after hearing how the king tried to destroy an entire port without hard evidence, Rannn agreed we did the *honorable* thing."

Her top fell to the ground, followed by her bra.

She saw the need in his eyes as he looked at her breasts, and she held her breath, waiting for him to touch them. But he didn't.

Gammon got on his knees and slowly unfastened her pants. "The Federation council sent scout ships to five of the planets they thought were uninhabited and found that all were inhabited. Incidentally, five new races have been added to the Federation archives."

Amaree smiled politely, not really interested in hearing any of it. But as his mate, she wanted to be supportive. "So, the Federation is not moving into the Outworlds?"

Gammon had her step out of her clothes before grabbing the mattress from the bed and laying it on the floor. Then he guided her down. Starting from her ankle, he pressed his lips against her skin while running one hand up her thigh. He was too far away to touch anything good, but knowing he would get there eventually made her burn even hotter.

Instead of moving to the next spot, he brushed his thumb over her inner thigh with one hand and told her, "The Federation is sending in terraformers to the Asaiah System to begin the expanse."

She knew the Cerebrals and Sarem Moon were in the Asaiah System. But she was having a hard time pretending to be interested when the movements of his thumb pulled all of her attention.

"That's nice," she said, a little breathless.

Gammon kissed the next inch of skin and the next until he made it to her inner knee. His hand was close enough to touch her lady parts but he instead begun brushing the very top of her inner thigh—a breath away from her scorching and pulsating sex.

"Rannn also..." he started as he pushed his thumb into her soaking core. She bowed her back as he massaged her deeply. He said something else, but she couldn't hear given the blood flowing through her body and pounding inside her, building her to a climax.

He stopped, and she growled at him. Pissed that he would dare.

Gammon's ears perked as he smiled. "You have no comment?"

"I commented," she snapped. "I am glad for the Federation."

"I wasn't talking about the Federation. I was talking about me."

Did he really want to have a conversation right now? What the hell? "Okay, what about you?"

Gammon clicked his tongue as he lowered to her inner thigh, nipped it, and then kissed it. "You don't seem to be interested. I can wait," he said, but everything in his tone said otherwise.

"No, I'm interested. What happened?" she said, trying very hard to concentrate on what he said and not him pulling her flesh into his mouth as he pushed his thumb back inside her channel and massaged.

He wasn't deep enough, and his mouth wasn't where she wanted it, but she reached for a climax anyway.

Gammon let go of her flesh and smirked, obviously feeling her trying to suck his thumb in deeper. The tempting bastard moved his mouth to the next spot and sucked in another breath as he began rounding her opening but not putting enough pressure on it to finish her.

She made a whining cry in the back of her throat and pleaded for him to stop teasing and playing.

Gammon let go of her flesh and moved between her legs. "Every time you're away from me..." he started and then dropped his mouth to brush his fingers over her sensitive flesh.

Her sex vibrated, and she felt close to climax yet not close at all. She was in a state of absolute carnal need.

"This is how it feels when you're not near me." Looking up, she knew he was checking to make sure she'd heard him.

And she did. Loud and clear. Being distant was bad.

"And this..." he started as he lowered his mouth and

consumed her flesh, working his tongue like a masseuse, getting into every crevice.

Her orgasm instantly began to build, hard and fast as she closed her eyes and dropped her head back. It would be huge if he ever let her reach it. Higher and higher it twisted and climbed. Just before it hit, Gammon pulled back.

"Noooooo," she said, reaching for him.

"And that is what it felt like when you left me."

Assuming he was talking about their mating, she said, "I didn't leave you. I would never leave you."

He stood up and spoke slowly. "You left the ship that was being attacked. By grace, you weren't killed. Then you ventured onto a deadly, class-three planet to join in on a battle."

Amaree genuinely felt bad and it combined with the insane need she felt to come by her mate's hands.

"I'm sorry," she said.

"No, you're not. You're just sorry you didn't come."

True, but also... "I'm sorry it did *this* to you. But I went because I felt needed. And on that planet, I was more than a doctor. I was...more. I can't explain it."

"It's okay, I can. You realized you could use your abilities in ways that you hadn't before. Add given the addictive nature of the adrenaline that comes from battle, you figured you're ready for a lifetime of action and adventure."

Being naked and irritated, she sat up. "It's not an addiction. It's more."

He grunted and took off his shirt, throwing it onto the floor. Unfastening his pants, he said, "All right, then will you need more of it? More danger? More doing things on your own? More choices that will give you a rush and beat me down?"

Amaree went to push herself up because this obviously was not a playful conversation. She was barely off the mattress when Gammon moved over her and growled, "Answer my question."

She licked her lips. "You're mad, and I get that. I did make some bad decisions, and I know now that they hurt you. And I'm sorry."

In the same voice, he told her, "I've been hurt my whole life. I'm not delicate. But you didn't answer my question, and I *need* an answer."

She hated hearing that he was brushing over the fact that she'd hurt him. She hated that she felt lumped in with his abusers. "No, I'm not going to do anything that will hurt you again."

He leaned down so that his mouth was just over her ear. His mouth brushed her lobe as he said, "You're telling me that if your cousin asked you to join his crew, you'd tell him no?"

She opened her mouth to speak, but his thumb brushed over her bud and began circling, perfectly assaulting her needy bits.

"Gammon," she whispered, confused and also desperate to let him know that she didn't want to hurt him. She wanted to be a good mate.

"This is what it feels like, hun," he said as he pulled his hand away and, in one smooth motion, entered her body, stretching her wider than ever before. He felt so big she gasped.

Pulling out, he rocked back in, shaking her womb.

"This," he growled as he slammed home over and over, rooting deeply every time, opening her to passion with sex that she didn't know existed. He bit her flesh. He held a handful of hair, keeping complete control of her head and her body as he took over and pillaged.

She was so wet, their sex was sloppy and loud, and her climax built back up. It grew bigger and twisted tighter, and Gammon never stopped.

Taking her hard, she held on as she finally reached her peak. Oh, Gammon had done it.

He'd taken her there.

Yes.

Yesssssss.

"GAMMON," she bellowed as her vision faded and all she could feel was the mile-high wave cresting and spilling over her, filling her with a heat that consumed her. Her lungs stopped working, and she felt as if she were drowning in pleasure.

She was lost.

Then she felt a spike of additional pleasure as he pinched her nipple and kept going. He moved her to her side and owned her body. He took her from behind and finally said, "This is what it feels like when I'm in battle."

He was insatiable and unstoppable, and she was at his mercy. He took her to another orgasm before he finished violently. Then, he held her down and forced another climax out of her with his hand. All the while, he whispered in her ear how much he needed to feel her cum again...and again.

Her body was completely sated when he finally let her go. She didn't move, and her breathing was labored. Her eyes had closed, and she didn't have the energy to open them again. But she heard him when he said, "Rannn also officially retired me from the Federation."

That's what'd caused this.

She reached for him. "You're afraid I will want adventure now that you're ready to retire? That's why you're mad at me."

"No, hun, I was mad because I don't want you to leave me. I want thousands of years with you, and I can't have that if you aren't safe. I know you're strong and skilled, but I will always worry," he said as he began brushing his thumb over her lady parts.

"I can't go again," she whispered.

"You will," he said confidently. "But more importantly, do you want to stay with the Maw?"

Her legs dropped open at his ministrations, and she wished that her body wasn't so damn responsive with his every touch.

"Hun, I need an answer."

"I don't want to answer wrong," she said.

"Answer honestly, then," he said as he moved down to her nipples and began licking them.

"Yes," she said to everything he was doing *and* to wanting to stay with the Maw.

"Yes? You want to stay with the Maw?"

"Yes," she said again, even more breathless.

Gammon moved until his face was between her legs. He kissed her swollen lips and said, "Then we'll stay on the Maw, and you'll promise never to leave without telling me. Understood?"

He didn't give her a chance to say anything before his mouth did things to her that made her completely primal—knowing only his body.

Long after that night, she would realize that he was mixing their scents and mating her so deeply that she would smell him on her for the rest of her life. Her life had changed so quickly, and yet she wouldn't change a thing. Gammon had kidnapped her heart and soul. Her parents were not happy, but they accepted her decision.

Life on the Maw was always intense and dangerous, but in their cabin, when they were together, the universe didn't matter, and their love was infinite.

EPILOGUE

The New Mission

Amaree sat on a medbed, reading the white papers on the progression of rehabilitation therapy. Everything about the topic seemed to be something that took a long time.

She hoped not. Her Yunkins deserved a better life than watching over her.

The door to the medical bay opened, and Amaree smiled, happy to see her mate.

Gammon jerked his chin at Motis, who dutifully watched over her. "The fighting slaves...I mean survivors have been transferred."

"That's good," she said, setting down the Minky pad and expecting that this was his way of telling her that they were about to go to their cabin.

"You want to know what's better than that?"

She nodded, again thinking about their room.

"King Azze reached out to Fenton, asking if she took contracts."

Really? "What did she say? What kind of contract?" Amaree's stomach fluttered at the possibility of another mission.

"The pirate queen leaked the king's allergy to a general, who doesn't like the king. The general challenged Simmer, threw powdered mellow-whatever at him, and then stabbed him in the heart."

Covering her mouth, Amaree felt so bad for the king.

Gammon pulled her wrist down and said, "Simmer's body was taken to the king, and the general attacked him with the same stuff."

Oh...no.

"Azze kept the medscope on him, so he didn't suffer and was able to kill the general *and* save his son. But now, he's pissed."

Her blood began to buzz as she asked, "The king wants us to catch the pirate queen?"

Gammon held up a finger. "To destroy her empire."

"Honestly, it's for the best."

Leaning close, Gammon brushed his lips over hers. "Yes, it is." When she leaned in, and he broke the kiss, she growled.

"Rannn also gave Fenton another mission."

Groaning, she doubted it would be as exciting as destroying a pirate queen's empire. Gammon shook his head at her, but with a warm look in his eyes said, "I love your savage side."

She couldn't say the same back to him. But she did say, "I love it when you look at me like that."

"Are you saying you don't love my savage side?"

"I respect your savage side. I know that you can always keep me safe, but it's not my favorite part." As she said that, she remembered all the things he'd done to her flesh, and she blushed. Forcing herself to turn away from her lust, she said, "I love how perfect you are."

His eyes darkened as he leaned over and used his bedroom voice. "Did I ever tell you what it feels like to love you?"

Oh...Seth.

Her body was literally conditioned to that voice. Her heart started to pound, and she already itched to jump off the bed and run to the cabin.

"It's complex and will take hours to explain."

Oh...help.

Taking her by the hand, he led her out of the bay and down to their room. As soon as they were inside, he crowded her against the wall. Before he kissed her, she said, "I love you. Every part of you, even the dark bits. I love all of you."

Emotions deep and murky crossed his eyes whenever she said she loved him. He had no problem saying that he loved her, but when she'd first said it, he'd had a hard time with it.

He knew that she wanted to be his mate and that she was bonded, but he mistook her need for him for how good he was in bed. For the last two months, she'd made it her goal to heal the part of him that felt unworthy.

"I love you, too," he whispered and brushed a thumb over her cheek. Then he stepped back and reached into his pocket, handing over a small cloth bag. Something looked even more off with his expression, so she was hesitant to take it.

Opening the drawstring, she saw a rose gold chain. Turning the bag over, she let the chain fall out into her hand. Feeling it in her fingers, though, she realized it was stronger than gold. Much stronger. And it didn't respond to her like her frostic knife.

"What is this?"

"A marriage gift."

A what? A wedding gift?

"Your race marries. I didn't know if you'd want a ring, but a ring didn't encompass all of you. And I love all of you."

Amaree's eyes started to mist. "This is better than a ring. By far."

Gammon took in a breath and began silently undressing her.

He turned her around to face the wall as he took the chain. There was something so fragile about it but she couldn't imagine why. He draped the thin but weighted trinket around her neck. A lighter stream of chain bounced off her spine as he fastened the clasp.

Then, he took the larger loop and brought it around her stomach, wrapping his arms around her as he did. When he finished, he pressed his lips to her shoulder and then pushed the button on the wall that doubled as a mirror.

He turned her around and had the mirror freeze the image so when she turned around, she saw little drops inscribed with their names in an infinity symbol.

"I love this," she said once she'd turned around again and touched his chest. "It's you and me. Forever."

His forehead dropped to hers. "Forever."

---

10 Years Later - Port Nicca
There Once Was A Goat

"Amaree," called a male from the other side of her office door. She didn't recognize the voice as one of her staff from the hospital.

"Come in," she called and swiped her fingers across the screen to minimize the file of a medbed order to replace the old ones.

The door opened, and a red Kingling walked in with his hand around the back of her son's neck. She leaned forward and covered her mouth, praying to Seth of Stars to give her patience from whatever she was about to hear.

Her son kept his eyes downcast, but she didn't smell any remorse. The Kingling pushed the boy in and pointed at him, accusing, "He ruined my entire herd, and I demand vengeance."

She dropped her hand. "I don't—what herd? And what did he do to it?" Praying more, she hoped that her son hadn't kidnapped a herd of animals or creatures. It had taken years to break Nebo of that, and she knew that Nebo and her son were almost always around each other.

"My goats."

Goats?

Crap.

She held up her hand to let him know that she would pay him for all the goats her son had taken—and probably ate with her sneaky-ass bodyguard.

"He trained my goats to attack me."

"He...really?" Leaning back in her seat, she wasn't exactly sure how to repay that.

Her son whipped around and boldly declared, "I taught them to defend themselves. I figured if you're going to slaughter them, they should at least have a fighting chance."

Amaree's heart hurt at hearing the emotion in her son's voice. Her husband thought he was old enough to understand why his protectors didn't talk. When Gammon was done explaining, her son went quiet for a day.

Since then, he had been getting in trouble a lot more.

"Those goats are animals, and animals don't have brains. They don't talk, and they're good for one thing," the Kingling spat, but was cut off when her son growled viciously as he lunged.

Amaree reached out mentally and stopped him, then floated him back to her. To the Kingling, she calmly replied, "I will buy your goats. That way, you can take the money and buy a new herd."

"Agreed," said the Kingling, who eyed her son. "But if you come around my animals again, I will deal with you myself."

"Looking forward to it," her son snapped, and she froze his mouth, too.

The Kingling snorted as he turned and left. Once he was gone, she figured that her orders would have to wait. Letting her son down, he folded his arms and stomped to the door. She opened it with her abilities and saw Motis leaning against the wall, picking at his nails.

"I'm going to take Harun home to his father and let him know that we are now the proud owners of attack goats."

Motis nodded.

Remembering that she had a small request to ask of the Yunkin, she winced. "Human Amy switched shifts with Jarrik again. She will need someone to walk her home. Last time she went by herself, she fell on a stray-nettle cactus and ended up blind for a week, and my mother called every day to check on her. I'd like to avoid those calls if I can help it."

Motis never showed more emotion than when she brought up Human Amy. Taking an annoyed breath, he said, "Fine."

In all the years she'd known him, only Amy got that reaction. Human Amy had an anti-aging chip, and Amaree was sure it also stunted her mind because the female was a walking disaster. But by the grace of Seth, Amy did something for Motis that no one in all the galaxies could do. She got him to react. Maybe, one day, Motis would start living for himself...and see if the tension between him and Amy could be something more.

ACKNOWLEDGMENTS

First I want to thank the Lord for guiding me when life and a story's plots go awry. Second, I want to acknowledge my two alpha readers Evon and Jan, who have the tolerance to read my early drafts. They have become my dearest friends and I consider them a blessing. Third, I want to extend a special thanks to my beta reader Amanda who always asks the right questions. My books would not be possible without a team behind me.

I also want to extend a heartfelt thanks to my editor Chelle, Literally Addicted to Detail for making my stories shine.

I want to give a shout out to my Facebook followers who read my non-edited stories and choose-your-own-adventures. Without them, Nem and Pasha's story would never have been created and this series wouldn't be the same without them.

Last but not least, you, my reader for reading this story. Regardless if you liked it or not, I hope you leave a review. An honest review gives me the feedback I need to write the stories you love.

MORE BOOKS BY LAYLA STONE

Click here to read the next book in the Unusual Pirates Series

Click here to read Nem and Pasha's story for free.

Click here to read more books by Layla Stone.

To hang out, find me on **Facebook**

To get a notification when a new book comes out check out my **Bookbub**

If you like pictures of sci-fi characters, worlds and spaceships check out **Instagram**

Join my newsletter if you want to get an inside look to what I'm working on, what's coming out and what I'm planning in the future. **Monthly Newsletter**